DESPERADOS

Other books by Art Isberg:

Fontana
Resurrection at Medina
Vengeance at Quiet Creek

DESPERADOS

•

Art Isberg

AVALON BOOKS
NEW YORK

Published by Avalon Books,
an imprint of Thomas Bouregy & Co., Inc.
160 Madison Avenue, New York, NY 10016

Library of Congress Cataloging-in-Publication Data

Isberg, Art.
   Desperados / Art Isberg.
      p. cm.
   ISBN 978-0-8034-7655-4 (hardcover, acid-free paper : alk.
paper)   1. Outlaws—Fiction.   2. Montana—Fiction.
I. Title.
   PS3609.S28D47   2011
   813'.6—dc22

                                        2010037666

PRINTED IN THE UNITED STATES OF AMERICA
ON ACID-FREE PAPER
BY RR DONNELLEY, BLOOMSBURG, PENNSYLVANIA

To all those young men who started out against the odds
but beat them before they were beaten

Chapter One

School Days

A young boy came running into the classroom in the back-woods Montana schoolhouse shouting for help. "Mrs. Thompson, come quick! There's a fight out in the schoolyard. It's Trey Wingo and Johnny Blades again. They both got bloody noses!"

The portly schoolmarm grimaced, turning from the chalk-board to rush outside where two boys were rolling on the ground in a ball of dust, throwing punches. "Trey, Johnny, stop this fighting right now. Do you hear me? I said stop it!" She grabbed the lanky sixteen-year-olds by their collars, yanking them to their feet as each kept their hands cocked and ready to throw another punch. Other kids crowded around wide-eyed, talking excitedly.

"I want to know who started this! Who threw the first punch and why? Speak up. Which one of you is to blame?" She scowled, but kept her stare on Trey for good reason.

He'd been an incorrigible kid since his first day of school five years ago. Being eleven years old and the oldest in the class hadn't helped either. But his mother and father hadn't been able to get him to attend class earlier, no matter how hard they'd tried. Trey's mother, Samantha, explained that he was an odd sort of kid and might need special attention. Mrs. Thompson had no idea what she was getting into and tried to help. Well, she sure did now and had just about given up on him and his troublemaking ways.

Johnny finally lowered his hands, wiping his bloody nose on the back of his shirtsleeve. "I ain't saying who started it."

"What about you, Trey? I'll tell both of you right now, your folks are going to hear about this and I mean today! I've had just about enough of both you boys always disrupting my class. Will you answer me or not?"

Trey's eyes were still focused on Johnny, but all he did was shrug and reach into his overalls for a handkerchief, then mop a trickle of blood from the cut on his face. At sixteen years old, the tall, blue-eyed kid towered over Mrs. Thompson. He had no respect for authority of any kind, including her; however, he idolized his father because of his tough, bare-knuckles up-bringing and independent attitude. Kip had drifted from job to job, quitting after ending up in some kind of dispute with the people he worked for. That's when he picked up his family and moved west to Montana to his own homestead. If he was al-ways going to break his back working, he figured it best if he did so for himself and his family instead of someone else.

"All right, I'm sending both of you home with a note to your parents about your deplorable behavior today. Your an-tics and fighting with the other boys has gotten so bad, it makes my teaching almost a waste of time. I won't have it anymore, do you understand me? I won't!" She glared at each of them. "You're being suspended until next Monday. Maybe if you've got the weekend to think it over, you might come to your senses. Now get inside while I write these notes. The rest of you children stay out here until I call you back into class."

Both teenagers stood at her desk as she wrote, staring at each other. She didn't see the small smile play over Trey's face then vanish before she finished. "Go home and think about what you've done, the both of you. You'd better come to your senses if either of you have any. Now get out of my sight until next Monday. One more time like this, and you can stay gone for good!"

Outside, the pair headed for their horses tied out back. As they passed, one of the other boys chided Trey. "Boy, are you gonna get a whippin' when you get home and your mom and dad read what Mrs. Thompson wrote."

"Don't worry about it, you little snitch. Just don't let me catch you walking home, or I'll give you a bloody nose too." He shoved the kid off balance with a hand to his face and kept walking until he reached the horses.

After mounting up, they kicked their animals out of the schoolyard as the rest of the class watched them go. Mrs. Thompson came out and shook her head in despair. Turning back to her students, she said, "You've just seen two boys who are going to get into nothing but trouble for the rest of their lives if they don't change their ways. Please don't any of you children emulate their behavior. I want all of you to grow up and become decent young men and women. Recess is over. Let's get back inside and start our arithmetic test."

Trey and Johnny streaked through rolling hill country at a breakneck pace, wildly racing each other to see who would be first to reach the ford at Copper Creek three miles ahead. First Johnny was in the lead, then Trey passed him, riding flat-out bareback and flashing a big grin.

The teenagers were already accomplished, daring horsemen. The more reckless one rode, the more the other tried to top him. But it was Trey who thought up the trouble they always got themselves into. He had a wicked imagination that bordered on scary. Almost as bad, Johnny was just stubborn enough not to back down on a dare. Together they got themselves in and out of one scrape after another, and school was no exception. Their parents' homesteads were just a few miles apart, and they'd become fast friends as kids. Both also considered themselves too grown up to waste time in school studying history, mathematics, and other boring subjects.

Trey came flying into the ford first, yanking his heaving mount to a stop in shallow riffles, looking back as Johnny topped a low rise, splashing in moments later. "You cheated." Johnny jerked a thumb over his shoulder. "You cut through the trees instead of staying on the road."

"Don't cry about it," Trey taunted him. "I never said we had to stay on any road, did I? Besides, my little plan at school worked like a dream, didn't it, just like I said it would? We got out of class and didn't have to take that math test. If it wasn't for me, we'd both be sitting back there listening to Mrs. Thompson ask us a bunch of dumb questions we don't know the answers to."

"Well, there's nothing wrong with knowing some things. You don't want to grow up to be an idiot, do you? I mean, I'll bet you don't even know who the president of the United States is. Everyone should know that."

"I do know who it is. It's Polk. And I know something else too. He ain't done anything for your folks or mine. Look how they have to struggle just to keep food on the table. So what good does it do to know who the president is three thousand miles away who don't give a dang about us or anyone else way out here in Montana Territory?"

Johnny was stymied for a moment. Trey always came back with some fast answer or comment. In his own way he knew Trey was a lot smarter than most people thought, even if he didn't get it from school books. He let the discussion pass, delicately rubbing his sore jaw.

"Listen. Next time you dream up some way to get us expelled, do it without me getting a bloody nose over it, will ya? Maybe we could just put a skunk in the outhouse or something like that?"

"It got us out, didn't it?" Trey glanced back with that devilish grin of his.

"Yeah, but now we've got these notes to our folks. My dad is going to skin me alive when he reads it. So is yours."

"No, they ain't." Trey took the folded paper out of his pocket and tore it into tiny pieces, letting it drop into the water. It was carried away by the dancing current. Johnny smiled and shook his head, following suit. "And I'll tell you something else too," Trey continued. "I ain't going back to school next Monday or ever. I'm going to ask my dad if I can stay home and work the ranch with him and my brother, Frank. If that don't work, maybe I'll ride to town and get some kind of job. I've had all the schooling I want. What I need now is to make some money. I'm tired of having nothing, and I'm tired of seeing my folks the same way. I know one other thing too. I can't make a dime sitting in that classroom with a bunch of snot-nosed kids. I'm done with it."

Johnny didn't say anything for a moment, searching Trey's face for some sign he was kidding. Slowly he realized that his friend was dead serious. "You can't do that. Your folks won't let you just quit and stay home. You better think about that, boy."

"I already have. I decided a long time ago I was done with school. You should be too. We're just wasting time riding there every day. Think about it, Johnny. What good does it do? You get a piece of paper saying you showed up. What's that worth? My own pa can barely read his own name, but he's got a horse ranch started, and he didn't need no school to do it either. I can already read and write better than he can. I'm heading home. I'll see you later, and it won't be in no schoolyard either!"

Johnny sat watching Trey ride away. He wondered what his pal would think up next. Whatever it was, he'd try to join in and keep up. That's the way it was. Trey dreamt up some wild scheme, and Johnny followed to show he wasn't chicken.

Samantha Wingo stood by the kitchen window as she fixed dinner. Her once-pretty face was now lined with the hard labor of struggling alongside her husband, trying to make his horse ranch a reality. At thirty-nine, her long chestnut hair was already streaked with gray. The hard labors of three children, all boys, hadn't helped either. One child died at birth. Trey and his older brother, Frank, had survived the rigors of Rocky Mountain winters, growing up wiry and tough just like their father, Kip. Their hardscrabble life clearing timber and building a large log house, barn, and corrals did not yield easily to the hand and hopes of man. It had taken a toll on all of them, especially Samantha.

Samantha, Kip, and the two surviving boys had left their home in Kentucky eight years earlier to come west to try and carve out a new life for themselves and what they'd hoped would be new opportunities. At times like this, when she was alone with her thoughts, she wondered if it had all been worth it. Had they really made the right decision? She would never voice that concern to Kip. She loved him too much to ever give him one moment of doubt. He'd vowed to struggle until his last breath to make their dream come true against the Montana wilderness. She meant to see that happen, no matter how hard it was on her.

She stopped arguing with herself long enough to look out the window. Trey was riding toward the house. What was he doing home so early? she wondered. Then she felt that familiar gnawing in the pit of her stomach telling her that he'd gotten into some kind of trouble again. She'd always placed a lot of value on him getting a decent education. Neither Kip nor Frank ever had the chance to finish school. She was the only one in the family to complete grade school and even high school. Kip trusted her judgment implicitly, and she kept all the ranch records and ran money matters. All her hopes were pinned on Trey getting an education, but it'd been an endless struggle trying to keep him in school. He'd always been the wild child, yet she never gave up hope.

He reined to a halt, tied off the horse, and headed for the front door. Before entering, he stopped to take in a deep breath. He knew what was coming. This wasn't going to be easy, but he wasn't going to back down now. He pushed the door open and stepped inside.

Samantha was already there, hands on her hips, the concern on her face obvious. "Please don't tell me you're in trouble again, Trey. What are you doing home so early from school?"

He gave her a big hug, holding her in his strong arms as she tried to push back and get an answer. Nearly six feet tall, already he was taller than her. His best weapon against questions he didn't want to answer had always been to hold her close so she couldn't admonish him face to face.

Art Isberg

"Trey, let me go so I can talk to you," she insisted. "It won't work this time. Now stop this, and tell me what happened."

In one quick motion he swept her off her feet and carried her into the big room near the fireplace, gently lowering her on the stone hearth and sitting beside her.

"There's no trouble, Ma, honest. And there isn't going to be any either, if you'll just listen to what I have to say."

"That's just what I'm afraid of." She stared back slowly, shook her head in despair.

For the next half hour they argued back and forth, but Samantha could see it was a battle she would not win. In desperation, she tried to reason with him one last time.

"You're throwing away something so very important. Can't you understand that, Trey? You say you want to stay home and work the ranch with your father and Frank, or if that doesn't work, get a job someplace? Doing what? Can't you see how we've struggled just to keep what little we have here? Do you think you can just ride out into the world and make any kind of real money? For God's sake, listen to reason, Trey!"

"Ma, listen to me. Let's talk to Pa when he gets home. I think he'll want the extra help. It'll make things easier all the way around, you'll see. I know about horses and how to work the ranch, and I didn't learn that in any school either. There's some things they just don't teach in books, and how to make a living is one of them."

"Your father isn't here right now." She got up, walking behind him and placing both hands on his broad shoulders. "He and Frank took some horses down to Loyalton for sale. They won't be back for at least another couple of days."

"Loyalton? Why didn't Pa tell me they were going? I could have helped out and went along."

"That's exactly why he didn't tell you. He knew you'd want to miss school. Both of us want you to finish school, and I'm sure your father will tell you the same thing when he gets back. When are you going to listen to reason?"

Two days later, Trey was out at the corral repairing a saddle when he looked up to see a rider coming in. At first he thought it might be Johnny, but as he got closer he realized that wasn't Johnny's horse. He called out to the house for Samantha, and she came outside just as the stranger pulled to a halt.

"Hello, folks," the rider said as he dismounted. "I was told this is the Wingo place. Is that right?"

"It is," Trey answered. "I don't remember seeing you before."

"Well, no, I reckon not. I live in Loyalton. I've come a fair piece just to find you. I'm afraid I've got some bad news for you, ma'am. The sheriff sent me up here to deliver it."

"What kind of news?" Samantha's eyes widened in concern, and she clutched her apron.

"Well, it looks like your husband and son were held up and robbed after selling some horses back in town. There was a gunfight and . . ."

"What's happened?" Samantha voice rose as she gripped Trey's arm to steady herself.

"The sheriff figures they put up a fight. Your husband was shot and killed, ma'am. Your boy was wounded but he's alive and the doctor is taking care of him at his place. I'm awful sorry to be the one to have to tell you this."

Samantha collapsed in Trey's arms. "Quick, mister, open the front door," Trey ordered. "I've got to get her inside!"

Once in the house, he gently lowered Samantha in a chair,

then hurried to the water bucket and wrung out a cloth. Back at her side, he placed the damp cloth on her forehead. "How bad is my brother?" he asked the messenger.

"Doc says he took a bullet in the shoulder and one grazed his side. He got the bullet out of his shoulder, but he'll have to rest a while before he gets back on his feet again. Sheriff Gibber says when you folks come to town he has your dad's gear in his office. Both horses are down at Ladd's Livery Stable. I guess you'll have to arrange for your dad's burial too, unless you want to bring him back here?"

"You tell the sheriff I'll be coming in as soon as I can get someone to take care of my mother. I don't want her riding all the way there to see that. I want to see my brother, Frank, as quick as I can too, and find out what happened and who he thinks did this."

"Okay, son, I'll tell him. There aren't any other adults that can come with you, is there? I mean, you might be a little young to have to take all this on by yourself."

"Don't worry about me. It looks like I just became the man in this family, at least for now."

Trey made Samantha as comfortable as possible, promising he'd be back as fast as he could after riding over to the Blades ranch to ask Johnny's mother if she could stay with her while he rode for Loyalton. An hour later, he was explaining what happened to everyone.

"My God, Trey! How could something like that take place?" Rachel Blades' hands came to her mouth. "Oh, poor Samantha. I've got to get over there just as quick as I can. Howard"— she turned to her husband—"get the buckboard ready. I'm leaving as soon as I can pack a few things."

"You riding to town alone, son?" Howard questioned, putting a hand on Trey's shoulder. "That's a pretty big load for anyone to carry, let alone a boy like yourself."

"I've got no choice. Besides, I want to see my brother, Frank. I don't know how bad off he is, only that he was shot twice. If you want to let Johnny ride with me, I could use the company."

"I don't know about that, Trey. There's already enough trouble brewing without getting him into it. I know you're in a world of hurt right now, but I'm not sure that's such a good idea."

"Oh, Howard. The Wingos are our best friends." Rachel stepped forward, gently putting a hand on her husband's shoulder. "Let him go with Trey. He'll only miss a day or two of school, and it's almost over for the year anyway. He needs Johnny's support and company. Please, I think it's the least we can do at a time like this."

Howard looked at his wife, then Johnny, weighing his thoughts for a moment. "If your mother thinks it's all right, then I guess you can go. But I want you to get your tail back here as soon as you can after things are settled. And I want both of you to ride with your mother back to the Wingo ranch before you leave for town. I don't want her out there in the buckboard alone in the dark. And once you get into Loyalton, you both remember to stay out of trouble, you hear?"

Chapter Two

Loyalton Justice

 $\mathbf{B}$ ack at the ranch Samantha placed a leather billfold in Trey's hands. Her hands were shaking with emotion as she did so. "Try not to spend any more of this than you have to. I don't have much more here to fall back on now. After you take care of your father and see Frank, get yourself back home. I need you here more than ever now." She cupped his face in her hands and tears ran down her cheeks. He pulled her close, asking her not to worry. He promised he'd take care of everything.

Suddenly he was the man of the family. Now he had to act like it. He'd vowed to quit school and grow up fast, but he never dreamed it would happen like this.

The two young men rode steadily throughout that night, rarely saying a word as the tragedy of events swirled around Trey and emotion consumed him. As they galloped through tall timber trees under a full moon, Johnny glanced over once to see tears streaking his friend's face. He said nothing, and they rode on.

When dawn painted the eastern sky in wisps of filmy gray,

Johnny called to Trey, "Don't you think we ought to give these horses a rest? We've been pushing them pretty hard all night."

They pulled to a halt at the next small stream, getting down to stretch their legs as the horses drank eagerly from the cool water. When Johnny glanced at Trey again in the growing light, the pain he'd seen earlier was gone. In its place was the grim look of seething anger as he paced back and forth, nervously kicking at the dirt. "If we keep up this pace we should reach Loyalton by dark. I want to see Frank as soon as I can. Let's get going."

They rode into town that evening to find the livery stable on Main Street. The owner, Jay Ladd, had closed for the day and was in his house in back of the corral. Trey rousted him out explaining that they wanted to leave both horses. He told him to give them a good feed until morning when they'd be back and asked where the doctor's office was. Ladd told him it was one block over from Main Street. Then Trey asked about the sheriff.

"He's likely over at the Buckhorn Bar right about now. He props up the counter over there every night after he closes his office and makes the rounds."

Doctor Feeney looked up from a book and adjusted his glasses, heeding the loud knocking at the front door. He was tall, skinny as a rail, and wore wire-rimmed glasses perched on the end of his nose. He looked more like a bookkeeper than a doctor. But he'd proved to be dedicated to his profession, delivering babies; patching up cuts, bruises, and broken bones; and even taking care of farm animals when the need arose. When he opened the door, he was surprised to see two strapping teenagers standing there. Trey quickly introduced himself and Johnny, explaining that he'd been told his brother, Frank, was there.

"Oh, yes. He mentioned you before I worked on him. He said you'd come as soon as you could. I didn't realize you were so young, though. Come in."

Feeney led them down a hall, talking over his shoulder at a whisper. "He's lost a lot of blood with two bullet wounds. I got it stopped after removing the lead and sewing him up. He'll need a lot of bed rest before he goes anywhere. My wife fed him some hot soup about half an hour ago, so he might be asleep. If he is, I don't want to wake him. Bed rest is the best medicine now."

The doctor stopped at the door, putting a finger to his lips before turning the handle and stepping quietly into the room. He motioned Trey to follow, but Johnny stopped at just looking in. Frank's eyes were closed. His breath came in congested heaves as they walked closer. At the bedside, Trey looked down. His brother's whiskered face looked pale, gaunt, and almost deathlike. Trey had always admired his big brother, but now he looked small and fragile. A lump of emotion stuck in Trey's throat. He tried to clear it before leaning down closer.

"Frank, it's me, Trey. Can you hear me, bud?" Trey whispered.

Frank's eyes flickered open, trying to focus on the young face hovering above him. Very slowly he raised a hand and gripped Trey's shirtsleeve. He tried a weak smile but couldn't hold it. Trey wrapped both his hands around his as tears filled his eyes.

"You're gonna be okay. Doc Feeney says so. What happened, Frank? Tell me if you can."

"They . . . got . . . Pa. Damn near . . . me too."

"Who did it, Frank? Did you recognize any of them? Doc says you can't talk too long, so just tell me the best you can."

He shook his head slowly back and forth. "Don't . . . know

any of them. But I got a bullet . . . in one of 'em. I think his leg. He went down . . . but they picked him up. The leader rode a big bay horse . . . with a white star on his forehead. I don't know about the others."

Trey straightened up, his face seething with emotion. He lowered Frank's hand onto the blanket. "You just rest easy. I'll be back in the morning. Get some sleep now."

At the front door Trey shook hands with Doc Feeney and thanked him for all he'd done. He promised to pay for his brother's care as soon as he sold his father's horse and saddle. That's when Feeney told him Kip's body was at Skinner's, the undertaker's office on Main Street. He also suggested the Placer King Hotel, if both boys wanted someplace to stay for the night. All Trey wanted to know was the location of the Buckhorn Bar. Feeney told him it was at the other end of town on Main Street, but that they couldn't drink, if that's what he had in mind.

"I don't want any liquor. I want to find this sheriff of yours, Gibber. Thanks again, Doc. I'll be back tomorrow."

George Gibber was leaning against the bar counter swirling a shot of whisky around in his glass, studying its amber glow. For a Friday, it was surprisingly quiet. Usually there was a small crowd, if you call a dozen men a crowd. Only three other men stood at the far end of the bar, with another four at tables scattered around the room. The sheriff was in his midfifties. He'd been elected eight years earlier in a town that rarely needed one, except to steer a Saturday-night drunk over to the two-cell jail to sleep off a hangover.

The gold strike that originally fueled Loyalton's surge of new inhabitants had petered out years earlier. The first word of a gold strike was carried around the country like a northern gale. Men came from out of nowhere, pulling mules loaded with packs—some wearing everything they owned on their backs, others in high-topped hats who had never dirtied their hands in their entire lives—to spin the fickle wheel of fortune at gambling tables and faro houses. They packed up when the golden veins did, heading for the next place promising quick riches, like lemmings to the sea. The quiet country was left to a few scattered horse and cattle ranches trying to eke out a living in unforgiving mountains, surviving Montana's bitter winters until grass came back again in the spring.

The sheriff was not a physically big man, and his dress didn't help. His tall, crowned cowboy hat was perched atop a thin mound of snow white hair. The tin star pinned on his vest was faded and scratched, almost too big for his shirt. His striped pants were tucked in knee-high boots that made him appear shorter than he actually was. He was not a figure to inspire confidence, but the town didn't mind. Loyalton had seen its heyday. Now it was content to rest in past glory.

Sheriff Gibber tipped up the glass, sliding the last of the amber liquid past a full mustache, then nodded for the barkeep. "Top this one off, Sam. Then I'm turning in for the night."

As the baldheaded owner started to pour, his eyes went past the sheriff to Trey and Johnny, who were coming through the front door. "Hey, you two can't come in here. Get yourself back home and wait until you get some whiskers before you come back. Go on, now."

The sheriff turned to see the pair of young men ignore the warning and continue toward him. Sheriff Gibber put the glass down. "Didn't you hear what Sam just—"

"You Gibber?" Trey cut him off. The sheriff nodded. "My name's Trey Wingo. My father was robbed and murdered and my brother shot outside your town a few days back. I rode in here to find out who did it, and what you're doing about it."

The lawman appraised the pair with growing contempt as customers put down their glasses to hear his answer. "This ain't no time or place to talk about that. I open up the office at eight tomorrow morning. You show up, and I'll give you your father's personal belongings. I've got them in my safe. Now get out of here like Sam just said."

Trey stepped closer. He was taller than Sheriff Gibber, and the officer had to look up at him. There was no mistaking the rage he saw in the young man's eyes. "Why aren't you out after the men who murdered my pa? My brother is laying half dead down at the doctor's office. Instead, I come in here and find you sucking on a whisky glass."

Sheriff Gibber suddenly pushed Trey back, his face turning red at being called out in front of everyone by a teenage kid. "You watch your mouth, sonny, or I'll lock up you and your friend until you learn to show some respect. Those four hold-up men, whoever they are, aren't from around here. There's no one to lock up. They were just drifters passing through. By now they're likely fifty miles away, and my legal jurisdiction ends right where town does. I can't go after four men on a wild goose chase and leave town without any law. So don't try and tell me my job. Now get out of here!"

The barroom was dead quiet. Everyone watched, wondering what would happen next. Johnny took a step back, afraid Trey might throw a punch. He'd seen his short fuse go off enough times before. Neither man moved, locked in a standoff. The sheriff saw the kid wasn't going to back down and finally decided to try and defuse the situation before it got any worse.

"Just to get you and your friend out of my hair, I'll unlock the office and get your father's gear for you. But I want you two out of town by noon tomorrow. If I see you on the street after that I'll lock you up, you understand? Get your business done and go back where you came from. You're nothing but trouble looking for more of it. I run a peaceable town, and I mean to keep it that way. Now follow me, and make it fast."

Inside the office, Gibber lit a lantern, then dialed the safe combination over in one corner. He came back to the desk, laying out Kip's sale papers, empty leather billfold, cartridge belt, and six-gun. Trey fingered the objects, tight-lipped, before looking up.

"Where's my dad's rifle?"

Gibber turned, pulling it down from the wall gun rack. "This is everything he had on him when we found him. I don't know if Skinner, down at the undertaker's parlor, has anything else or not. You'll have to ask him when he opens in the morning."

Trey asked about his father's vest chain. It had a five-dollar gold piece on it. It was his lucky charm. "This is everything we took off him, like I said. You can ask Skinner about it when you see him. His horse and saddle are down at Ladd's. Just remember I did you a favor even bringing you over here tonight. Don't push your luck. Now get out of my sight and cool down before you end up in real trouble."

The next morning, as the first rays of sun bathed the dirt streets of Loyalton, Isaac Skinner came striding down the boardwalk toward his funeral parlor. As he drew closer, he saw two young men standing by the front door eyeing him. Skinner looked exactly like the profession he'd chosen. Short and bony in an ill-fitting suit, his clothes hung on him in deep creases. His black hat and string tie framed a gaunt, hairless, milk-white face. He nodded hello as he came to the door.

"What can I do for you two young men so early in the morning?" he asked, reaching for the front door keys. Trey explained that he was Kip's son. "Oh, yes. I've got Mr. Wingo in back. He's all fixed up for you too. I figured someone would be coming to take him to glory, so I took the liberty of going ahead and preparing him without asking. I guess no one is better than a man's own seed. Come in. I'll take you to him."

Skinner led them through a front display room of wooden coffins, pulling back curtains leading into a second room. The place had the smell of death to it even before he lit a candle stand next to the coffin. Trey stepped forward in the flickering glow, his hands clutching the side of the casket. He looked down at his father's face, which was frozen in death. It didn't look like his father anymore. His knuckles began turning bone white as he gripped the wooden sideboards.

Skinner leaned close, whispering in his ear. "You may kiss him good-bye, if you like. It's all right. He looks like he's just sleeping peacefully, doesn't he? I did a real nice job for you and your family, if I do say so myself."

Trey kept staring at the body. His hands moved down just once to touch Kip's cold face. Then he turned to Skinner. "No, he looks dead to me. Close him up. After I sell off his horse and saddle, I'll settle up with you. You see to it he gets a decent burial and good headstone. I want it to say *Loving husband of Samantha, brave father to sons Frank and Trey. We'll meet again in glory.*"

"Aren't you going to be here to take care of all this?" Isaac questioned.

"No." Trey slowly shook his head. "I'm going after whoever did this to him. The law around here sure as hell won't, and somebody's got to. You just do what I said. I'll pay for everything."

Later that morning, Trey and Johnny went back to visit Frank. Frank had just finished breakfast and was more alert.

Trey explained he was going to sell off Pa's horse and gear, then pay off the stable owner and the undertaker. He told Frank to ride back home and take care of their mother as soon as he got well enough. Frank's eyes narrowed with concern. "Isn't that Pa's gun belt you're wearing? Where do you think you're going with that?"

"I'm going after the men who killed Pa and shot him to pieces. I even have a description. The leader rode a horse with a white blaze on its forehead," Trey told him.

Frank said he thought the man wore a large black hat with a silver concho hatband, and he'd also hit one of them in the leg. Trey told his brother that the local sheriff wasn't going to do a thing about it. "The law don't care about people like us, Frank. To them we're just a bunch of ranchers living out in the sticks."

Frank begged him to wait until he could get back on his feet, promising they'd go together. One man alone didn't stand a prayer of taking down four gunmen. Still, Trey was determined, telling him that there was no time to wait. The killers would only get farther away, so he had to move and move fast. He reached down, running his hands through Frank's thick dark hair. "You just tell Ma I'll get back home soon as I can and not to worry, okay? Remember what Pa always said, Frank? Anytime anyone leaves boot prints up your back, be sure you do the same. Pa's laid out cold down the street. Now I'm going to leave our boot prints up someone else's back. Take care of yourself and Ma too. You tell her I'll be back home soon as I can. Tell her I've taken care of Pa, and tell her I love her no matter what happens. I'm gonna make everything all right or die trying."

Chapter Three

Eagleville

After selling his father's horse and gear, Trey paid off everyone. Then he turned to Johnny, putting a hand on his shoulder. "Listen, bud, it's time you headed back home. I don't expect you to be a part of this from here on out. You tell your folks and my mom why I'm not coming back with you. You'll be there before Frank does, that's for sure."

Johnny locked eyes with his boyhood pal. The fun-loving days of school suddenly seemed far away. Trey meant to kill someone. You could see it in his eyes. Something had changed in him almost overnight. He'd become a man, and a deadly one with a purpose. He meant to avenge his father's death and nothing would stop him.

Johnny's mind raced with indecision and fear. The easiest thing to do was just saddle up and ride for home, like Trey said. Yet something stopped him, scared as he was. He knew his pal didn't stand a hoot or holler in hell of going up against four men and coming out alive. Maybe, in his own strange way, Johnny had grown up too.

Johnny swallowed. His mouth was dry until he found his

voice. "I'm not going home, at least not yet. I'll ride to Ea-gleville with you and see if we can find these men."

"You better be sure about this. There's going to be gunplay if I find them. This isn't you and me back home going out buck hunting. I mean to kill 'em, Johnny. You think you can really do that?"

Johnny nodded slowly. They'd been friends too long for him to let Trey just ride off alone. He couldn't live with that if something happened to Trey. Johnny would go through with it even though he was scared stiff. A slow smile parted Trey's lips and he slapped Johnny on the back. "Okay. Let's get to it then."

Eagleville was the nearest town, twenty long miles away through high-timber country. Neither Trey nor Johnny had ever been there. They'd heard their folks talk about how much bigger it was than Loyalton, and that it was the hub of mining and timber business. After Loyalton's placers had run dry of yellow iron, Eagleville's golden veins still held the promise of fantastic riches for any man with enough luck, grit, and backbone to sink a shaft in the right spot. Trey had a hunch it might hold something else too: the killers of his father.

It was well past midnight when the pair topped a high ridge, pulling to a stop to look down on Eagleville. Tiny pinpoints of light danced below from kerosene lanterns. Johnny asked Trey if they were going to ride into town, and Trey responded that they'd sleep up here and go down in the morning light. They unsaddled their horses, tied them off, and made a quick, one-blanket bed on pine needles. Johnny fell asleep quickly, but not Trey. He lay awake staring up at frozen stars, planning how he'd face the killers, if he found them. He shivered from the cold, not fear. He was ready to kill someone.

When the icy dawn rose, Trey awoke, staring up at the thick canopy of pines overhead. He decided their first stop would be the livery stable to inquire about a blaze-faced horse and four riders. A town as big as Eagleville had to have a doctor, maybe even two. He'd head there next to ask about anyone treated for a gunshot wound in the leg. Reaching under the blanket, his hand rested on Kip's .45 caliber wheel gun. Fingers wrapped around the graceful curve of cold, walnut pistol grips. It was his gun now. He'd make the killers pay while using it. Rolling over, Trey pulled at Johnny's blanket. "Hey, it's time to get up. Let's go."

Even though the morning sun barely cleared the ridge tops surrounding the town, people were busy on the sidewalks as the pair of young men rode down Eagleville's main street. Trey searched the side streets until he saw the livery stable sign and turned in.

The gray-haired proprietor, Lum Hooten, was working on a saddle as they pulled to a stop. "You young fellers looking to stable your horses?" He eyed them up and down, wondering if they could afford it.

Trey told him they might, but first he needed some information.

"Like what?" Hooten's eyes narrowed. He wasn't inclined to do anything for anyone if he couldn't turn a dollar. At this early hour he wasn't much in the mood either, especially for a couple of strange teenagers who looked like they didn't have two bits between them.

Trey told him he was looking for a man who rode a blaze-faced horse and came in with three other riders. "You seen anyone like that in the last three or four days?" he asked.

"Maybe, maybe not. What's it worth to you?" Hooten hooked both thumbs in his suspenders, looking from Trey to Johnny and spitting out a stream of tobacco juice.

"This isn't a game. Just give me a straight answer, yes or no!" The sudden anger in Trey's voice was real. The stable man saw it, and he pursed his lips and took a step back. He didn't want to let some kid buffalo him, but this kid was six feet tall and wore a hog leg on his hip. He finally admitted he had a horse like that out back in the corral.

Trey asked if the rider had come in with anyone else. Lum admitted there were three other men, but only one paid for all four animals to be put up.

"What did he look like? Can you remember anything, clothes, hair color, things like that?" asked Trey.

Lum pulled at his scraggly beard, squinting. He had lots of people come through with all the miners and other strangers drifting into town. All he really paid any attention to was what they had in their wallets, but he did remember one thing. The man was tall, had black, curly hair, and wore a wide-brimmed hat with a silver concho hatband. A bolt of electricity shot through Trey. The killers were here. Now all he had to do was find them.

"If you mean to make some sort of trouble, maybe it'd be best if you went to our sheriff and told him about it." Hooten could see the look on Trey's face. He knew the kid wasn't searching for old friends. Trey shook his head and asked where the doctor's office was. The proprietor gave him directions, then stood watching the pair as they saddled up and rode away. He'd already made up his mind. If Sheriff Lawrence Todd came by, he'd mention the strange conversation and his strong feeling that trouble could be brewing with these two young men.

"Why yes, I did have a man in here with a gunshot wound to the leg." Doctor Lane nodded in his office. "It was up high, but the bullet went clear through and didn't break bone. He was lucky. I cleaned it up and stitched him shut. He won't be riding anyplace until I take the stitches out. He'd likely bleed to death if he tried. Why do you ask? Is he a friend of yours?"

Trey shook his head, but he wasn't done asking questions. "Do you remember anything about what the man looked like?"

The doctor said he was sort of short, had curly red hair, and was with three other men who waited outside until one came in to pay him for his work.

"Was the money man wearing a black hat with a silver hatband?" Trey questioned.

Doc Lane's face lit up. "Why yes, he was wearing a hat like that."

"Did they say anything about where they might be staying?"

"No, not that I recall. But when he comes back here to get the stitches out I can ask, if you'd like."

Trey thanked the doctor for his help and told him he might be back later if he couldn't find the men on his own. When he and Johnny left, Doc Lane went to the window, watching them saddle up and ride back toward town. He wondered what the strange conversation was really about, then turned and went back to his work.

Trace Taggart sat in a chair on the second floor of the Timberline Hotel with his feet propped up on the windowsill, staring down at the street below. He was impatient and irritable. His plans had been stalled. Bart "Red" Chinn was laying in the bed behind him in long johns, his leg wrapped in heavy bandages. Red had to heal up before he and his pals could saddle up and leave town, and Trace was edgy. So far the robbery and killing back in Loyalton hadn't caught up with them, but the longer they stayed here the greater the chance the word could spread and the law might come looking for them. If the local sheriff got wind of it, they'd have to shoot their way out of town with a cripple slowing them down.

Red pulled himself up into a sitting position with a groan. "When's Jack and Harlon gonna get back with somethin' to eat? I'm half-starved to death. They've been gone nearly an hour already."

Trace spun in the chair, glaring at him. "Shut up, Red, and stop your whining," he shot back. "If you hadn't went and caught a bullet, none of us would even be here. We'd be a hundred miles away like we're supposed to be. Instead, we're all stuck in this hole because of you. And I'll tell you something else too. If you ain't able to ride in another two days, I'll leave you here and we'll clear out on our own!"

Red sank back down in the bed, clutching the steel rail headboard tight with both hands. He knew Trace wasn't kidding. If they abandoned him now, the law might catch up and he'd hang alone. The pain in his leg throbbed even worse thinking about it. He laid back staring at the ceiling and kept his mouth shut.

Jack Lambert and Harlon Holmes came strutting down the boardwalk toward the Timberline carrying a paper sack with biscuits and beef jerky. The quick glances passersby gave them before looking away made it obvious neither man was a local rancher or miner dressed like that. Lambert, tall and slim, wore fancy gambler's clothes. He packed a six-gun on each hip, a sure sign he was a gunny and not a working man. Jack liked the looks of fear he got from other men because of his attire and heavy iron. Holmes was shorter, heavyset, and grim-faced with a bulldog jaw. He carried his wheel gun butt forward in its holster for a cross-draw pull, maintaining it was faster. Their unshaven faces and dark eyes under their wide-brimmed hats made it plain they were not to be messed with by anyone, even the law.

Trace and his pals had been highly successful in a series of bank robberies and store holdups in several small towns in plains country at the foot of the mountains. It was Trace's idea to ride up here into high country for a while to let things cool down. Robbing and killing Kip and Frank outside of Loyalton hadn't been planned. They saw the pair bringing horses into town. The next day they ran into them again leaving without the stock. Trace quickly concluded they'd sold the animals and must be carrying cash from the sale. They jumped the pair after leaving town, and a vicious gunfight took place. They thought both men had been killed, leaving no witnesses.

After walking around town most of the afternoon, Trey and Johnny had seen no one matching the sketchy description. They found a side street bench under a shade tree and sat talking about their lack of success. The killers' horses were still stabled at Lum Hooten's, so they had to be in town someplace. Maybe, Trey reasoned, if they didn't show during daylight, they might come out after dark. Johnny nodded, adding that it might be smarter if they went to the sheriff and let him in on what they knew, but Trey immediately nixed the idea. He'd seen all the law he wanted. He'd asked the law for help once, and once was enough. But, he added, if Johnny didn't have the stomach for it, he could still ride for home. Johnny glanced at his boyhood pal and shook his head no.

When the sun sank behind the timber-topped ridges surrounding town and long shadows crept across the dirt streets, Trey gave Johnny his rifle, holstering Kip's six-gun for himself. They lingered outside of Lum's until full dark, then started for Main Street. Lanterns were lit inside saloons and gambling houses. The evening crowd was beginning to filter in as the pair reached Main Street. Trey stopped at the first watering hole, peering through the window at the men inside, one by one. He could easily see all were working men, with dirty clothes and unshaven faces. *Probably miners,* he thought, looking over at Johnny and shaking his head. They moved farther down the boardwalk.

Just three blocks away, on the second floor of the Timberline, Trace slowly got to his feet and stretched. He'd been cooped up all day in the room listening to Red complain. Now he was thirsty and wanted out. "I'm going down to the hotel bar and get myself a drink. Anyone want to go with me?"

Red immediately spoke up, but Trace cut him short. "You ain't going nowhere," he shot back. "You stay right here. If any law does show up, you're a dead giveaway. I ain't taking that chance."

Red sank back down in the squeaky bed as Jack and Harlon got to their feet. "We'll go," Jack said, strapping on his gun belt. "I'm about bone dry, sitting around here all day long. Let's go wet our whistles."

Chapter Four

Street Fight

The three men walked through the lobby where a desk clerk was busy reading the paper. He nodded as they passed. At the saloon entrance Trace stopped, scanning the room carefully for any sign of a badge. He was a careful man. That's why he was the brains of the outfit. He didn't take chances. Their robberies had been well planned. They'd gotten away with each one without a scratch, except for Red. The big oak bar was already half full of men involved in animated conversation. The tables scattered across the rest of the room were filling up too. He glanced back at Jack and Harlon, jerking his head toward the bar.

Outside in the dark, Trey and Johnny had worked their way down one side of the street, peering into gambling houses and noisy barrooms without success. Their nervous tension built with each failure. Shadowy figures that passed them on the boardwalk didn't notice the rifle Johnny had hidden under his coat. Now they approached the big, red-lettered sign hanging in front of the Timberline Hotel. Trey came to a stop, peering through another smoke-stained window.

The room was busy with men drinking at the bar and tables. His steady blue eyes went from man to man. Nothing. He moved left to get a better look farther up the bar. Suddenly he stiffened, grabbing Johnny by his coat and pulling him alongside him. The flash of a silver concho hatband blinked back. "That's him." Trey's voice was a low whisper. "See the two standing next to him? I remember we passed them on the street this afternoon. That makes three, but there's one missing."

Johnny took in a deep breath. He'd almost hoped they wouldn't find them. His hands trembled, tightening on the rifle stock. "How are you going to call them out?"

Trey looked around the darkened street. Across from them was the black shadow of an alley. Instantly, he had an idea. He told Johnny to go over and stand just inside the alley where he had a clear view of the street. "I'll go inside and call him out. If that doesn't work and all three come out, you open up on the other two while I take the big man. Are you ready for this?" Trey stared hard as his pal. Johnny nodded without answering, turning to start across the street.

Trey pulled the six-gun, rotating the chambers to be sure all six cylinders were full. Then he pushed through the front door of the Timberline and walked into the barroom. No one paid any attention to the tall young man as he worked his way through the tables toward the bar lined with drinkers. Twenty feet away he stopped, calling out above the noise of the room.

"You, concho hat, step away from the bar!"

Everyone in the room stopped talking and turned toward the young man. Jack, leaning on the bar, twisted around to look over his shoulder. "Is that kid talking to you?" he asked Trace.

Trace put down his glass, turning to face the kid. A quick glance told him he'd never seen him before. "What do you want, boy?" he asked.

"You robbed and killed my father back in Loyalton. Shot down my brother too. Step away from the bar. Now you're gonna get yours."

A slow smile came over Trace's face. He knew no kid was going to outdraw him, especially with Jack and Harlon at his side. He wasn't about to admit to any killings in front of all these witnesses either. He decided to just bluff the kid and back him down.

"You got the wrong man, sonny. You go back home before that big mouth of yours gets yourself killed. Go on, get out of here."

Trey didn't move an inch. Jack and Harlon squared up on each side of Trace, their gun hands dropping belt high. For several seconds the silence was deafening.

Spectators quickly got up from their tables, moving up against the wall out of the line of fire. Several others headed for the door, while men at the bar moved back too. In a matter of seconds, the four men had the floor to themselves. Outside in the lobby, the desk clerk heard the commotion and came to the door. One quick look was all he needed to turn and run out the front door for Sheriff Todd's house three blocks away.

"I want you out in the street," Trey ordered. "If you don't come out, I'll come back in here and take you right where you're standing. A lot of other people might get shot up that don't need to. I'll give you three minutes to show yourself."

"We don't need this, Trace," Jack whispered. "We've already got Loyalton on our backs. Let's just get Red and clear out of here before the law shows up."

Trace's eyes swept the room of customers staring back at him. His mind spun with indecision. Would he cut and run from a teenage kid, or let his natural instincts take over? He glanced at Jack and Harlon. They saw the answer in his eyes.

"I'm not gonna run from some snot-nosed kid calling me out in front of everyone. He started it, and I'm gonna finish it. Are you two coming with me or not?"

The three walked across the room to the front door, checking their pistols as they went. Trace edged around, looking outside into the street lit by lantern light. Trey was standing in the middle of it, waiting. Trace looked at his pals. A slow smile came over his face. "Soon as I finish him off, we'll get Red and clear out. I was leaving tomorrow anyway. Let's make it quick."

They stepped onto the boardwalk then down into the dirt street, spreading out as they came to a stop. Trace was slightly out in front. His voice was cold, hard, and confident. "I told you to get on home while you had the chance. Now they can carry you there in a pine box, boy."

Trey's heart pounded in his chest. He took in a deep breath, steadying himself, squaring up against the trio as his hand moved until fingers touched the walnut pistol grip. He had one last question. Now he asked Trace for the answer. "Are you the bastard that killed my father, or was it one of the scum with you?"

A slow smile spread over Trace's face. "Being that you ain't gonna get one day older, I'll tell you. Yeah, I took him down. He was slow, just like you. Make your move, sonny. I'm waiting to see how good you think you are!"

Trace's hand went for his wheel gun but the kid was faster, the black barrel of his .45 already clear of the holster, spitting a spear of yellow flame once, twice, three times.

Trace shuddered from the impact of the bullets, sagging to his knees with his mouth open as a spittle of blood ran down his chin before falling face-first into the dirt. Jack and Harlon opened fire as Trey threw himself onto the ground, rolling to fire back as rifle shots thundered out from the alley behind him. Jack cried out, spinning backward with his gun flying through the air. Harlon saw him go down and turned to run. He didn't get far.

Trey emptied his six-gun at the fleeing gunman while Johnny kept on firing until Harlon crashed down onto the boardwalk, twitching in his death throes.

For a moment the entire scene grew deathly quiet, thick smoke hanging on the nighttime air like an acrid, blue cloud. Then Johnny was at Trey's side, wide-eyed and trembling at the sudden death they'd dealt out. His voice was a nervous whisper. "We better get out of here. Let's go, Trey, let's go now."

Both young men started running down the street into the night toward the livery stable, as a crowd poured out of the Timberline bar and surrounded the three bodies sprawled on the ground. Suddenly everyone began talking excitedly at the same time. One man marveled at the kid's lightning-fast shooting. Another allowed as how it took real guts for just one kid to face three hard-nosed gunmen like Trace and his pals. But a third shouted something else. He'd seen the flash of gunfire coming from the alley behind the kid. He was dead certain there was someone else backing the teenage killer.

The crowd was still milling around when Sheriff Todd and the hotel clerk came running up. The lawman knelt, rolled Trace over, then looked up at the men milling around him. He asked if anyone knew the dead man or his pals. No one did, but everyone tried to explain the shootout at the same time. Sheriff Todd stood, holding up both hands for quiet, ordering everyone back inside the Timberline bar where he could try to get some straight answers one at a time. He stopped a moment on the boardwalk and ordered the desk clerk to get the undertaker, Tobin Morgan, to pick up the bodies.

Inside, Todd sat at a table calling up witnesses one at a

time, trying to piece together the puzzle of the murderous shootout. The more he questioned each man, the more incredible the story sounded, even though everyone did agree on one thing: a teenage boy had come into the bar accusing Trace Taggart of killing his father, then had taken down all three men in the street singlehandedly.

Sheriff Todd pursed his lips. He knew something about professional killers. Wherever they went they made news, and none were anywhere near Eagleville. Vince Jardeen was down in Kansas, working for a big cattle outfit dispensing his own kind of gun law for his employer. Bart Helmes was somewhere farther west, working for a mining company, running squatters and claim jumpers off mine property with his famous pearl-handled six-shooter. "Bull" Braxton was reputed to be in jail for killing a deputy who had tried to arrest him.

Who could this unknown teenage gun twirler be?

Sheriff Todd didn't have a clue. But he did have a good description. The kid was tall—nearly six foot—had curly, light brown hair and blue eyes. No one in town had ever seen him before, so he wasn't a local boy. The sheriff pushed back his chair, letting out a sigh. He didn't have much to go on, but he did have a stack of wanted posters back in his office that he could go through. He doubted it would do much good, but at least he'd give it a try.

While the lawman was holding court in the bar, Red painfully hobbled down the back stairs of the hotel into the night. He was getting out of Eagleville and fast, bleeding stitches or not. He wasn't about to wait for the sheriff to connect him to Trace and the others. He'd heard the commotion out on the street earlier and saw the blazing shootout take place from the second-story window of his room. They'd be burying three pine boxes with his pals in them. He wasn't about to wait around to fill up number four.

Trey and Johnny made it back to Lum's, quickly saddling their horses and kicking down the back streets out of town. Half an hour later they pulled to a stop on a high point overlooking Eagleville, giving the horses a rest. "Where to now?" Johnny asked, out of breath.

"Home," Trey answered. "but I might not stay long. Everyone got a good look at me. No one saw you though. Keep your mouth shut, and you'll be all right. It's better that way anyway. I got you into this, maybe I can get you out too."

The next day the *Eagleville Gazette* came out in bold, black, blaring headlines: TEENAGE KILLER GUNS DOWN THREE.

Trey was no longer a wild schoolboy used to bucking authority. Now he was a wanted man, with posters sent out to every town and hamlet in Montana. Both lawmen and bounty hunters would be looking for him dead or alive. Before his young life had begun, a growing list of men would be dedicated to ending it.

Two weeks later, George Gibber sat back in his office chair with his feet propped up on a half-open drawer, studying the new wanted poster he'd just received from Eagleville. There was no drawing with it, but the description sounded a lot like that Wingo kid he'd tangled with over his father's killing some weeks back at the Buckhorn. The more he thought about it, the more he started to believe it might actually be the kid they were looking for. If he was right, a piece of law work like this would make the quiet town, and especially its undistinguishable sheriff, look pretty good. He remembered that Doc Feeney had treated the kid's brother, Frank. Sheriff Gibber headed for the good doctor's office.

"Why yes, I remember Frank Wingo," Doc Feeney nodded, after inviting in Sheriff Gibber. "He left here for home over a week ago when he was well enough to ride. If that bullet he took had just been a few inches over, his artery would have been severed, and I wouldn't have been able to save him. He's a lucky man."

Sheriff Gibber asked the doctor if he knew exactly where the Wingos lived. Doc pursed his lips, trying to remember, and then his face brightened. "I'm not certain, but I think he said their place was in the meadows up near Storm King Mountain."

"Storm King, huh? I just might have to take a little ride up there pretty quick. I'll see you later, and thanks for your help, Doctor."

Sheriff Gibber sent a boy out to fetch Jarrod Lowe, his part-time deputy, who lived five miles outside of Loyalton. He told Lowe they were riding to the Wingo ranch the next day, and that if his hunch proved right there might even be some trouble. Lowe, a big, hulking man, was not known for his brains. It was his size that made him formidable, even if there wasn't much to back it up. He stared at the sheriff at the mention of trouble.

"Well, you know I've got a woman and four kids back at the ranch. I didn't sign on to wear this here badge and get involved in a shootout. It was the extra ten dollars a month that did it."

A pained expression came over the sheriff's face. He explained that if Jarrod just followed his plans to question Trey Wingo and they took him by surprise, everything would go off without a hitch. He quickly added that if they could bring in the suspected killer, they'd get a raise in pay plus the notoriety that went with it. The deputy looked back, unimpressed. He still didn't like the sound of it.

He'd have good reason to back up his suspicion sooner than he ever imagined. It wasn't going to be Trey Wingo who would be brought back to Loyalton, roped over a saddle facedown like a sack of wheat.

Chapter Five

Run for the Sun

After Trey and Johnny arrived home from Eagleville, Johnny told his folks he'd been with Trey in Loyalton waiting for Frank to get well enough to ride again. But when Trey reached home, his mother immediately sensed something had changed about him. She couldn't put her finger on it, and Trey wouldn't give her any help. She just knew he was a different young man than when he'd left days earlier.

The first time Trey and Frank were alone in the barn, the younger brother admitted to the killings in Eagleville. Frank stared back, trying not to believe what he'd just heard. He put a hand on his brother's shoulder, slowly shaking his head. "Good God, Trey. You've put the law on you now for sure. Why didn't you let them take care of this once you found those killers? Now they'll be coming after you sooner or later. What about Ma, the ranch, you and me running the place now with Pa gone? Didn't you think about any of this?"

Trey didn't flinch, staring Frank straight in the face. "I told you I was going after them. Did you think I was talking through my hat? The law ain't going to do a dang thing about

Pa's killing. I saw that right off with Gibber. He's a waste of time. If they do show up here, I'll run for it. Maybe when things cool down I could come back. If that happens, you'll have to explain it all to Ma. I don't want to give her anything else to worry about with Pa's death still on her mind."

Frank shook his head and turned away, staring at dark timber above the meadows where the horses were grazing. He needed more time to think this through. Pa was barely cold in his grave and now his younger brother was a wanted man. Trey didn't tell Frank that Johnny was with him in Eagleville, pulling a trigger too. He'd promised Johnny he'd always try to keep him clear, and he meant it.

Two days later Trey was out rounding up horses from timber beyond the meadows when he saw a pair of riders approaching the ranch below. They were still too far away to make out, but he didn't recognize the horses. The hair on the back of his neck tingled with the electricity of apprehension. Pulling to a stop at the edge of the pines, he watched them ride in and dismount.

Samantha was working in her vegetable garden at the side of the house when she heard the horses. She got to her feet and walked around front to see who it was. The moment she saw the badges she thought it must be news of her husband's killers. Why else would Loyalton law ride way out here?

"Morning, ma'am," Sheriff Gibber greeted her. "Is this the Wingo ranch?" he asked, getting down with a grunt.

"Yes, it is. What brings you here, Sheriff?" She pushed back strands of hair from her face.

"Well, Mrs. Wingo, I actually made the ride to ask a few questions of your son."

"My son? Frank is in the house. I'll ask him to come out.

What do you want to question him about? Have you found out anything about my husband's killers yet?"

"No, ma'am, I mean your son Trey, and I don't know anything more about the men who murdered your husband."

The sheriff walked up, leaning on the hitching rail while eyeing Samantha. He began explaining his meeting with Trey when he first rode into town and its disagreeable results. Then Sheriff Gibber pulled out a folded-up wanted poster from his vest pocket and handed it to her. Samantha slowly read it, then looked up when she was finished. "What's this got to do with us?" she asked.

"I don't rightly know for sure. That's what I rode out here to find out. Is Trey around here?"

Frank had started to open the door when he saw the two lawmen out front, their dull tin stars shining in the morning sun. Just as quick he closed the door, and a bolt of fear for Trey shot through him. He limped through the big log house out the back door, looking up on the timbered ridge. Trey was at the edge looking down. He took a few steps forward, waving his arms, trying to get his brother's attention.

Sheriff Gibber was still out front talking to Samantha when he stopped for a moment and turned to Deputy Lowe. "Take a look around and see if you find the kid. Bring him back here if you do. Get to it."

Trey saw a rider come around the house, stopping a moment to look uphill. The man spurred his horse forward, coming through the meadow toward him. It must be the law, he thought. Then Trey saw his brother waving his arms and knew he was right. His hand went down and he lifted Kip's six-gun out of the holster, checking to be certain all six cylinders were topped with dull grey domes of bullet lead. He slid it back in the holster, waiting. He wasn't going to be taken anywhere by anyone, badge or not.

The deputy's big horse cleared the meadow until it reached the edge of timber. Deputy Lowe leaned down, trying to look through the copse of limbs and branches, just able to make out Trey's shadowy form mounted on the other side. Before he could say a word, a voice rang out behind the cover. "That's far enough."

Jarrod straightened up in the saddle. He squinted, trying to get a better look, then urged his horse forward, deeper into the trees. "You Trey Wingo?" he shot back.

"That's right, and you're on private property. Get yourself off it and take whoever that is down there with you. I won't tell you twice."

Jarrod pulled his pistol, edging closer. "You listen to me. You're going to have to come down and talk to Sheriff Gibber. He's got some questions he wants to ask you. Don't make me have to drag you out of here."

"You're not taking me anywhere." Trey stiffened, leveling his gun as the deputy pushed through the last limbs, pointing his pistol straight at him. Suddenly the pines shook with the explosive report of three fast shots, and the deputy was driven back off his horse, landing on the ground in a heap. He quivered slightly then lay still.

Samantha screamed at the sound of gunfire, turning to look up on the ridge as Frank took off at a hobbling run across the meadow, calling out for his brother. Sheriff Gibber, wide-eyed at the sudden shots, cussed out loud, climbed back in the saddle and took off around the house into the meadow, passing Frank who was still trying to struggle uphill.

"Jarrod! Are you all right?" he shouted, closing in on the

pine thicket and pulling to a halt. He got down, pistol in hand, and saw under the branches a body lying on the ground. Moving cautiously forward, eyes darting back and forth through the branches, he reached it, kneeling to roll it over. Three bloody bullet holes lined the deputy's chest, his lifeless eyes half open. Sheriff Gibber sat back on his heels, shaking with emotion. Taking off his hat, he ran both hands through his thinning hair. Nervous sweat ran down his face. It all happened so fast, he couldn't believe it. Even though the killer had fled, he knew for sure who it was.

Frank finally made it uphill, gasping for breath and his head down, exhausted, praying it wasn't Trey on the ground. "What"—he wheezed—"happened?"

The sheriff slowly got to his feet, staring at him with rage in his eyes. "Your brother shot my deputy! Now I'll see to it that he hangs, if it's the last thing I do, by God!"

"How do you know it was Trey? You didn't see who pulled the trigger, neither did anyone else."

"Who in hell else could it be!" Sheriff Gibber yelled.

"I'm saying you don't know for sure, any more than you know who killed our father and shot me," Frank countered, as the two stood staring at each other without blinking.

Trey was already kicking his horse away over the hills as his mind spun with indecision. The deputy drew on him first. He was only defending himself. But who would believe him now? His only choice was to get far away where he could think about what to do next. The Blades' ranch was only five miles away over the hills. He headed for it to tell Johnny about the shooting. He was the only real friend he had.

When Trey arrived, he hid out in timber until dark, afraid someone might have followed him there. When the glow of lantern light lit the windows in the ranch house, he started for it. At the front door he fought with himself whether to knock and go in or wait until everyone went to bed then wake Johnny at his window. The stars overhead were dancing on a velvet black sky, and the first cool evening breeze rustled through the mountains. Out back in the barn a horse whinnied. It seemed like dozens of other long, lazy, summer evenings. But it wasn't. There was a murder in the air.

Just when Trey decided to knock, the door handle rattled to open, and he quickly stepped around the corner of the building out of sight. In the glow of the open door he saw Johnny carrying a water bucket and heading for the well. When the door closed, Trey whistled to him. Johnny stopped, spinning on his heels. "Who's there?"

"It's me, Trey. I've got to talk to you. Head over to the barn."

Once inside, Trey explained Sheriff Gibber's arrival at their ranch and the shooting. Johnny listened wide-eyed, fear creeping over him about another killing. "You that sure he's dead?" he asked. "What if you only wounded him, maybe it wouldn't be so bad."

Trey told him he was certain. At that short range he knew his bullets had been center-chest hits, and that he was going to run for it because he couldn't stay around here. Johnny rubbed his temples, trying to think. "Run where?"

"Just as far away as I can get, maybe for a year or even more where no one knows me or anything about the shooting. They'll hang me for sure if they ever catch me."

The two young men stood in shadows talking a few minutes longer before Johnny made a startling admission. "If they catch up to you, they'll eventually figure out I was with you in Eagleville. I pulled a trigger too, remember?"

Trey shook his head, telling Johnny he'd never have to

worry about that, even if he did get caught and ended up with a rope around his neck. He would never involve his boyhood friend, and he meant it. But Johnny was adamant. He said it would come out sooner or later. The ranch house door suddenly opened, framing Rachel Blades. She stepped outside calling for Johnny. He quickly pulled Trey close, telling him not to leave but wait until dark after everyone else went to bed.

"What for?" Trey whispered.

"Just wait and I'll slip back out then."

Trey retreated to the pines sitting thinking about everything that had happened so fast. He knew there was no turning back for him. The killings couldn't be undone. Sixteen or not, he'd already been branded a murderer. He leaned his head back against the tree trunk and closed his eyes. His world was spinning out of control, and there was nothing he could do about it but take whatever came. His breathing settled into a steady rhythm as he tried to relax, the tension slowly draining away. He finally fell asleep.

The next thing he knew, Johnny was shaking him awake. Even in the black of night, Trey could see he had a blanket roll over his shoulder and was packing his father's rifle. His saddled horse stood feet away. Trey pulled himself to his feet. "What's all this gear for?"

"I'm going with you. I'm not going to stay here and let Gibber or someone else come riding in like they did you."

"You're crazy!"

"Not half as crazy as you are. I wrote my folks a letter explaining everything and how it happened to both of us. I told them to let your mom know too. I said we'd try and come back when things quieted down, whenever that is, and not to worry. Whether we like it or not, I guess we're desperados now, huh?"

Trey started to argue, but gave up. Johnny was adamant. He

wasn't going to stay and wait for the law to track him down. The pair saddled up and rode off into the night. Atop a rocky point overlooking the ranch they pulled to a stop. The house and barn were bathed in blue shadows. Both knew it would be a long time before either of them would see it again. Neither spoke. They didn't have to. Their lives were now in jeopardy from that moment on. They reined the horses around, riding off through timber further into the night.

Over the next two weeks, Trey and Johnny rode down out of the high country they'd always called home, into rolling hills and scattered farming country. The first town they came to was the little community of Wheatland, arriving there just after sunup. The dirt street was nearly deserted except for a few horses tied at a hitching rail in front of a small eatery. The sign over the door read MAY'S DINER. They'd finished off the food Johnny had taken from home days ago, and both were tired and hungry. Trey still had some cash left and wanted some real food, so they decided to chance it and go in.

The small café was surprisingly full once they stepped through the front door. Local businessmen ate breakfast there before unlocking their doors for the day. The horses out front belonged to local farmers and ranchers in town, rounding out the clientele. Trey and Johnny edged through the room to a table over in one corner. May herself, a big woman in her mid-fifties, came to the table wearing an apron. She already had two cups and a coffeepot in hand and began pouring.

"What'll it be?" She smiled. "We don't get many strangers in town. You two young men just riding through?"

Trey nodded, trying to avoid any real conversation. Johnny asked what she served.

May explained she didn't use menus because they only had

four choices, and she knew them all and so did everyone else. Johnny ordered biscuits and gravy. Trey said he'd have bacon and eggs, with the eggs not too runny. May smiled and headed back to the kitchen.

No sooner had both of them began to relax as customers around them buzzed with talk than the front door opened and a tall, slender man wearing a five-point steel star walked in surveying the small room for a seat. Several diners greeted him as Trey kneed Johnny under the table. Both pulled their hats down slightly as he came across the room to the invitation of two men sitting right next to them. "We've got a chair for you here, Les."

Trey and Johnny tensed as the lawman walked through, diners pulling out a chair right behind them. Trey slowly eased his chair around, turning his back toward the sheriff, while Johnny stared down at the table, a knot of nervous tension churning in his stomach. He didn't look up until May was coming toward them balancing their platters with one hand like a circus acrobat, hips swiveling through chairs and tables.

"Here you go. Ready for a refill on the coffee?" she asked.

Johnny looked down at the steaming provender. All of a sudden he wasn't hungry anymore. Trey glanced up, nodding for more coffee, seemingly unconcerned about their situation. "Better eat while you've got the chance," he suggested. "It might be a while before we get another good meal."

Halfway through, breakfast conversation at the other table turned to the killing of the deputy up in Loyalton. The young men could hear every word through the clink of coffee cups and utensils. "The telegraph says the gunman is just a teenage kid," one man was saying. "Can you imagine that, Les? What is the country coming to when people like that are on the loose?"

The sheriff assured his friends that the killer wouldn't get far. They already had a good description of him and even his name. He guaranteed the kid would slip up and when he did, someone like himself or another lawman would collar him. Les twisted in his chair, calling for May to bring the coffeepot over. He glanced around, and saw Trey and Johnny with their head down, busy eating. "If you don't get her attention, she only takes care of you when it's time to pay the check," he kidded. Neither of them laughed or even acknowledged they'd heard him.

They quickly finished, and Trey paid the bill at the cash register. Outside, Johnny walked around his horse, resting his head on the saddle a moment. His stomach was still tied up in knots. He told Trey he thought he was about to lose his breakfast.

"No, you don't, not here. You wait until we get out of town. We don't need any more attention paid to us. Let's go before that lawman inside figures out who he just ate breakfast next to."

They saddled up and rode steadily until they were well outside of Wheatland. The fresh air felt good across Johnny's face, and he started to feel better. He glanced over at his partner. Trey's face was an implacable mask. Didn't anything ever bother him? Johnny wondered. The whole time they'd eaten next to the lawman, Trey continued forking down his food like he didn't have a care in the world. Johnny knew one other thing too. Trey would never give himself up. His boyhood pal was no longer just a teenage buddy challenging authority for the fun of it. Now he could kill at the drop of a hat. It scared Johnny to realize it. And he also knew he could never be like him no matter how hard he tried. Sure, he'd left home with him on the run, but deep down inside he knew that day would come when he'd want to go back and even turn himself in to explain how the shootout in Eagleville had really happened and why. Johnny was a follower, and Trey was a leader. That would never change. The die was set from boyhood.

"Well, what do we do now?" Johnny asked. "I thought by the time we got this far south, we'd be in the clear. It looks like the whole territory knows about us, if they do in Wheatland."

"We get farther away. Maybe California. They got a big gold strike out there. We could get lost in the scramble."

Johnny didn't answer for a moment. California was a thousand miles away. Besides, he wasn't a miner, he was a cowboy, used to working stock and horses. He didn't want to wander that far from home. "Why don't we try riding south?" he countered. "My folks say there's a lot of country that way with few people living in it except maybe Indians."

Trey stared ahead at the high rise of desert mountains along the skyline. "We could try that, maybe. I don't fancy myself at the end of a shovel digging holes in the ground anyway."

Chapter Six

Got Religion

Trey and Johnny rode steadily south over the next four weeks, traversing the rolling sagebrush-dotted prairies of southern Montana Territory, eventually reaching the rugged desert mountains of Utah's Wasatch Range. Trey turned seventeen years old along the way, but neither of them celebrated it. Their cash was gone, and they'd been living on what they could kill with their rifles, a jackrabbit now and then and what few grouse they could find. One afternoon they stopped to water their tired horses from a small mountain creek. Trey looked around the endless high country, bringing up their lack of food and cash, if they ever found anyplace to actually spend it in. Johnny took off his hat and rubbed his forehead in dismay. Both were dead tired with aching bellies.

"If we ever get down out of these mountains, maybe we can find some people, a town or ranch, something with a dollar in it," Trey complained. "This high country can't last forever, can it? I'm beginning to think heading south was a big mistake."

Johnny shrugged and didn't answer. Maybe Trey was right.

Even he wasn't sure anymore. Finally he suggested they swing a little east where the mountains seemed to slant downhill.

Later that day, they rode to the edge of a cliff, pulling to a halt. The sight that met them seemed so unreal that all they could do was sit in the saddle and stare, taking it all in. Far below were stony buttes run out onto expansive flatlands, a desert lake shimmering in the sun like a million diamonds stretching away as far as the eye could see. Between the lake and mountains, tiny green plots of rich farmlands dotted the flats. Wispy tendrils of blue smoke rose from several log cabins. Johnny was the first to break the long silence.

"Now I know where we are. I heard my folks talk about it once. You and me might have even read about it in our geography books back in Mrs. Thompson's class."

Trey turned to him, waiting for an answer. "Okay, where are we?"

"This has to be the Great Salt Lake. That means we've crossed over into Utah Territory. There's nothing else like that. And those farms down there, they have to be Mormons. You know, they've got their own version of the Good Book, and it says they can have as many wives as they want."

"I don't care about no wives, but we could both use a real good meal. I'm about half-starved. Let's ride on down there and see what we can stir up." Trey's unshaven face broke into a slow smile for the first time in weeks.

Joshua Logan was working on watering a field when he looked up to see a pair of riders coming toward him. As they drew closer, it was obvious they weren't from other farms or ranches around here. Those six-guns bouncing on their sides and rifle scabbards made it clear they weren't Mormons either. When they reined to a stop, Joshua saw they were young men about his own age. He straightened up, leaned on his shovel, and flashed a smile. "Morning." He nodded, eyeing the pair, their horses and garb.

Johnny greeted him, saying they were real glad to finally find some people after their long trek south. Trey said nothing, his eyes wandering beyond the field to a ranch house some distance away. Johnny asked if he was right about the lake. Joshua admitted it was the Great Salt Lake, then followed by asking him how long they'd been on the trail.

"For over a month, and I guess my friend and I must be in Utah Territory," Johnny answered. Joshua said he was right about that too, explaining the ranch belonged to his mother and father, until Trey broke in.

"We could use something to eat and drink. We can even pay a little for it if you've got something over at the house."

Joshua invited them to follow him. His mother and sister were home, and they could fix a couple of traveling strangers a meal. But first he asked if he could see one of their guns. He'd always been fascinated by weapons, even though his father did not allow one in the house. Johnny pulled his rifle from the scabbard, getting down and handing it to him. Joshua slowly lifted it to his cheek, sighting down the barrel. "Bang," he said softly under his breath, admiring the weapon longingly before handing it back.

"My father says no hand gun is allowed in our house. You'll have to leave your weapons outside on your horses. He says we came across half a continent to find our own place, leaving violence and lawlessness behind us. I guess your folks don't mind if you own them though, do they?"

Johnny replied that they didn't and extended a hand, pulling the blond teenager up behind him to ride double to the ranch. All the way over, Joshua couldn't keep his eyes off their weapons.

When they reached the big log ranch house, Joshua's mother and sister were outside washing clothes in a tin tub. Both women stopped and dried their hands, as the three boys dismounted. Joshua explained that the pair of strangers were just riding through and needed a meal. His mother was a thin, prudish-looking woman with a suspicious face masked by a large bonnet. Her eyes darted from Trey to Johnny. Johnny's eyes immediately went to the girl, fifteen-year-old Laura, her blond hair curling out from under the same type of headpiece. The instant their eyes met she quickly looked away and followed her mother into the house.

Opal Logan wasn't thrilled that Joshua had invited two complete strangers into her home. She watched them unbuckle the guns they wore, hanging them over their saddle horns. She knew they were from "outside" before Joshua even had the chance to explain. She also knew her husband, Ezzra, would like it even less when he got home from town. Opal and Laura busied themselves fixing something to eat while Trey and Johnny looked around the interior, almost uncomfortable at being confined after so many weeks out in the open. The smell of real food helped ease their feelings.

While Joshua made small talk about their sudden arrival, Johnny couldn't keep his eyes off of Laura, following her every move around the kitchen. From time to time, she'd glance at the handsome young man with the jet black hair and green eyes and then quickly look away, embarrassed she'd been caught. Trey saw it too, kicking Johnny under the table to hint to him to stop staring.

"Beans, some beef, and bread is what we've got." Opal came to the table carrying a plate for Trey. "There's no coffee or tea. We're Mormons and don't allow it in our house." Before turning away she told Trey and Johnny that her husband,

Ezzra, was a strict, plainspoken man, and he'd likely ask them to leave once he got home from Salt Lake City.

Johnny was quick to answer her. "We really do appreciate it, ma'am. This looks mighty fine compared to those tough, old sage hens we've been eating. We'd be glad to pay you for your trouble, but we're just about broke. Maybe we could work it off for you."

Opal shook her head no, as Laura leaned down to serve Johnny's plate. He could smell the sweet perfume of her hair, she was so close. When she brushed his shoulder while straightening up, their eyes met and his face reddened at the touch of her. Even under the long brown dress and double-layered blouse, Johnny could see she had the curves of a young woman, the most beautiful woman he'd ever seen. Trey's boot dug into his leg again, finally breaking the spell.

That evening, Ezzra Logan's wagon rattled up outside, and everyone exited the house to greet him. The instant his eyes fell on Trey and Johnny, a scowl came over his bearded face and he looked to his wife for an explanation. Joshua was quicker, talking fast, filling in details of how the pair had come to be here. Before he could finish, Ezzra held up his hand to stop, staring at the strangers.

"My son has been told many times not to bring strangers into our house. As you can see he's learned little from my lessons. Now that he's chosen to disobey me, you two can make yourselves useful unloading this wagon. You two can sleep in the barn for tonight. Tomorrow I'll decide what to do with you. We live by the book of Mormon, which I'm sure neither of you has the slightest knowledge of. It teaches us that hands that avoid work are ripe for inviting trouble. I don't allow trouble in my house. Not from anyone or anything."

After a prayer and dinner held largely in silence, Trey and

Johnny headed for the barn to spread their saddle blankets, lay down, and discuss the odd situation they found themselves in at the Logans' ranch. No sooner had they stretched out when they heard the crack of Ezzra's belt and Joshua yelling in pain at the whipping he was taking. When it finally stopped, Trey rolled over to face Johnny. "If that old man tries that belt on me, I'll pistol-whip him until he can't stand up. Let's get out of here tomorrow."

Johnny countered that no one would ever think of looking for them here in Utah, in a Mormon household where they could finally get some rest, food in their belly, and also give the horses a good rest after their long flight south. If they spent a couple of weeks working around the ranch, so what? They didn't know where they were heading next anyway, and didn't have the cash even if they did. Why not just sit tight for a little while? Trey rolled back over. He said he'd think about it. Both young men grew quiet with their own thoughts before drifting off to sleep.

In the black before dawn the next morning, Ezzra came into the barn carrying a lantern. "It's time for milking. Get up if you want breakfast. No one lays abed in my house until the sun comes up." He reached down, pulling the blankets off both men. "I won't have slackers eating at my table for doing nothing."

Trey rolled over still half-asleep, squinting up and then out the door into the dark. "It's still nighttime, and I don't know how to milk cows anyway. Gimme back that blanket."

Ezzra wouldn't quit. He prodded them with his foot, berating them until Trey started to jump to his feet before Johnny grabbed him. "I know how to milk. Give me the lantern and that bucket. I'll go do it."

In the days that followed, both young men pitched in working around the ranch. For Johnny, it was easier because he could spend time close to Laura, but Trey complained and did as little as possible until one day Ezzra told him he was taking him to town. The old man was determined to give him some direction for his errant ways, and getting him alone seemed like a good way to do it. As they headed for Salt Lake City, he explained the Mormon beliefs and religion in detail, hoping to get through to his young charge. His words fell on deaf ears until he mentioned how every member of the church was expected to pay a portion of their income to the church. Trey immediately straightened up, looking at Ezzra with sudden interest.

"You mean you actually pay money to go there?" he asked, his mind fixed on the thought of real cash.

Ezzra shook his head and explained that they believed the Lord was entitled to a fair share of their labors because the church supported them as they did it. Trey just stared at him.

"Didn't your father and mother ever give you any religious upbringing?"

Trey shook his head. "My father was killed in a robbery back in Montana Territory. My brother was shot too. We had a town sheriff that wouldn't do anything about it. That's my upbringing. You say *everyone* gives money to the church?"

Ezzra acknowledged that was true. In that same moment, his passenger began to figure out where he was going to get his next road stake. All he had to was work out how. These sod-busting Bible thumpers just might make enduring Ezzra's endless orders for more work worth it after all. He told Ezzra he and Johnny should ride in with them next Sunday and attend church themselves, to see how it all worked.

"Good," Ezzra nodded, thinking he might have actually made a breakthrough in his incorrigible young house guest. "It's never too late to take the Lord into your heart. Look what He's given us right here in this wonderful land. It was nothing but a barren desert against a salty lake when we first arrived. I'll look forward to Sunday, and so should you."

Back at the Logan ranch, Opal kept Johnny, Joshua, and Laura busy doing chores and working the fields. When they were away from the house, Joshua told Johnny about how miserable he was with his father's constant tyrannical dominance over this family and especially the beatings he handed out to him. He confided he'd thought of running away more than once, but didn't know where to go if he did. He envied Johnny and Trey's freedom to travel wherever they wanted without having to ask anyone's permission. Then he stunned Johnny.

"When you and Trey leave, I want to go with you. I mean it, Johnny. I'm not staying here any longer than I have to. I want to see the world over those mountains instead of staying here and getting beaten with a belt every time I do some little thing wrong. You tell Trey that too."

Sunday morning everyone climbed in the wagon heading for town to attend church services. By this time Trey had explained to Johnny about his sudden interest in religion and why. It made Johnny uncomfortable to think Trey was actually going to try and rob the church. If that wasn't worry enough, Johnny told Trey that Joshua wanted to leave with them when they left. Trey said to forget it, that he wasn't going to wet nurse some Mormon farm boy because his daddy used a belt on him. He told Johnny to make it plain he wasn't going anywhere with them no matter what.

As the wagon rattled on toward town, Johnny sat back, worried about the way things were going until he glanced over at Laura. Her straw-blond hair couldn't be hidden under a bonnet tied under her chin. Her blue eyes stared at the fields as they passed, then for just an instant they darted to Johnny. A quick smile lit her face, and his heart skipped a beat. She had to know how taken he was with her. Why else would she smile at him? Everything was getting more confusing by the day. He almost wished they'd never stumbled onto the religious enclave. Laura was the only thing that made it worthwhile, but he was afraid to think of what might happen next. His fears would soon be realized.

Chapter Seven

Joshua's Other Face

Trey sat in the big cathedral with his thumbs hooked in his belt loops, amazed by the throngs of worshippers filing in. He didn't think there were this many people in the entire valley. They all looked alike, dressed in plain dark clothes. The children were all well mannered and scrubbed clean. He glanced over at Johnny sitting next to Laura. His hand was moving slowly down until it was just touching hers. The pretty young woman glanced at her father and mother, who were busy looking at the crowd. She quickly squeezed Johnny's hand and then returned hers to her lap, still staring straight ahead, as Johnny smiled and settled back in his seat as the service began. Trey scowled at his pal, but Johnny didn't see it. He was lost in happy thoughts of his own, right where he wanted to be, as close as possible to Laura.

For Trey, the long service seemed to go on forever, with predictions of fire and brimstone to all nonbelievers. He almost feel asleep until Ezzra nudged him to pay attention. Finally, near the end of the service donations were called for. This is what Trey was here for. He sat up straight, watching carefully to see how much money was actually collected and where it was kept. A large leather-bound box was passed up and down the aisles, growing heavier with each new row. When it reached Trey, he hefted it, feeling its considerable weight before passing it on to Ezzra. He was certain there was more than just a road stake inside. He glanced over at Johnny, a quick smile passing his lips. Johnny knew exactly what he was thinking and was still squeamish about it. He wondered how Trey could actually rob a church and think so little of it. After the box completed the rounds, the preacher and two altar boys carried it out of sight through a side door before returning minutes later to end the service.

For the next two Sundays the Logans, Trey, and Johnny continued to attend church after working at the ranch for the entire week. Trey still avoided as much work as possible, complaining about it when he was caught. When the third weekend approached, he planned to ride out after dark on Sunday night into town to hit the church and then keep riding south. The Mormons wouldn't know what happened for days, and by then he'd be so far away no one could catch up to him. But there was one big kink in his plans. Johnny had fallen hopelessly in love with Laura, and told Trey he wasn't leaving with him.

"Are you crazy? You can't stay here with her. She's only sixteen years old, and Ezzra will run you off the minute he hears it!"

Johnny wouldn't be cowed, not this time, not even by his best friend. "Listen to me just this once, Trey. I'm already tired of running from the law. How far can you go before you have to shoot your way out of another scrape or maybe even get killed yourself? I know you and your family got a raw deal from the law back in Loyalton. But we can't do this forever, or at least I can't. I know Laura loves me. We feel the same way about each other. I'll stay here and take whatever Ezzra dishes out. If it gets too bad, I'll take her and head back to my mom and dad's place. She can stay there after I turn myself in. If I have to go to prison, she'll be there when I get out. And don't worry, I won't tell anyone where you're heading. Besides, you've already got a new partner. Joshua wants to leave with you. Take him and you won't have to ride alone."

Trey was so thunderstruck that for a moment all he could do was stare with his mouth half open at his boyhood pal. How could Johnny be so dumb? He took a step forward, putting both hands on his shoulders to try to talk some sense into him. "The law will stick your neck in a noose and pull it tight, don't you know that? What do you know about love anyway? You never even had a girlfriend before. Besides, I'm not taking some Bible-thumping kid with me as my partner. You're my partner, remember?"

Johnny wouldn't budge. Not this time. He'd made up his mind and he'd stick to it no matter how much Trey tried to change it. Laura made everything different. If Trey couldn't understand that, he couldn't help it. The battle of wills lasted only a few minutes longer until Trey got tired of trying to talk some sense into his pal. He walked away, shaking his head and talking to himself.

That next Sunday night out behind the barn, three figures stood in the shadows talking. Trey tried one last time to talk Johnny into leaving with him, but it was no use. He looked long and hard at his boyhood friend and stuck out his hand. They gripped each other while he told Johnny that he hoped he knew what he was doing. "It's not likely we'll see each other again, Johnny. We've been pals since we were kids. I guess I never thought it would end like this, especially not here. Take care of yourself. You're going to need all the help you can get when the law gets their dirty hands on you. They never will me. I'll never give them that chance. If I go down, it'll be with guns blazing."

"You do the same." Johnny nodded. "I hope they never find you after all this settles down somehow. Watch your back, Trey. You've got Joshua to help you now."

Trey and Joshua climbed into their saddles, riding away into the night as Johnny stood under a rising moon watching them go. He couldn't help but wonder where Trey would meet his end. He knew it would happen, and he knew Trey probably knew it too. All he could do now was hope it would be a long time before that day dawned. Trey was like a brother. He was almost blood to Johnny. He turned back, heading into the barn. Tomorrow he knew he'd have to face Ezzra's rage when he discovered Joshua had left with Trey. He didn't relish the thought. There was going to be hell to pay come sunup.

The pair rode down Salt Lake City's main street to dark and deserted streets. At the far end of town near rising hills, they reined to a halt behind the big church building down in the shadows. After tying off their horses, Joshua felt around for the back-door key hidden under the steps. Retrieving it, he opened the door and both men stepped inside. It was pitch black and deathly still save their own hesitant footfalls. They felt their way down a narrow hall until they reached a door. Joshua turned the handle, and they stepped inside a large room where he retrieved a candle holder. Lighting it, their ghostly shadows danced on the walls as the room glowed in flickering yellow.

"I think they keep it over here." Joshua started for a big cabinet on the wall. All doors were locked, so Trey took a poker from the fireplace, using it as a pry bar on one lock after another until he found the one containing the leather-bound box. They carried it to the desk and opened the top. The candle's glow lit a heavy pile of gold and silver coins, which filled the box nearly halfway to the top. Trey smiled. Maybe his new-found partner might work out all right after all.

As they exited the room, Joshua asked Trey to wait. There was something he had to do, and he'd never get another chance to do it. He led him farther down the hall through another door until they stood in the main cathedral. Shafts of moonlight filtered through tall stained-glass windows, giving the big hall an eerie, kaleidoscope glow.

Joshua walked up to the rostrum with both hands on his hips, looking around the huge hall. He may have felt a tinge of guilt for what he was about to do, but the sense of freedom he longed for trumped that feeling. The rules, restrictions, praying, and obeying were all behind him now. He was free at last, raising his hands up high over his head.

"Damn this place!" he shouted, the words echoing off shadowed walls, until he turned back to Trey. "I've wanted to do that for a long time. We can go now."

The duo rode steadily south through limestone mountains and plateau lands for the next three to four weeks until they reached Arizona Territory and the wide open frontier town of Mesa. The streets were filled with wagons, riders, and people busying themselves on the boardwalks. The thought of real food and a decent bed instead of a saddle blanket lying on the ground had Trey feeling upbeat. No one would know them here. They could take a break from running and enjoy life for a while. They pulled to a halt in front of the Desert Trading Post, and both swung down.

"It's time I got myself a pistol. This rifle of yours is too awkward on the street. Let's go inside and see if they've got anything." Joshua nodded toward the front door, as both men mounted the steps going in.

A bespectacled man in a bowler hat looked up over his glasses, eyeing his first customers of the day. "Howdy, gents. What can I do you out of?" He made a small joke as the pair came to the counter to look at several rifles in the gun rack on the wall behind him. Joshua asked if he had any pistols, and the proprietor pointed down to a beautiful pair of pearl-handled six-guns snuggled in dual holsters under the glass counter.

"Pull 'em up. I'd like to see them up close. How much?" Joshua asked.

The owner explained that they were top-quality weapons for which he had paid a large sum to the widow of the man who once wore them. His name was Jim Hart. He went on to explain that Hart was a well-known federal marshal and the only law within a hundred miles in any direction. He'd been ambushed and killed by *comancheros* he'd been trailing who were wanted for murder in Indian Territory.

"I'd have to have at least . . . fifty dollars American."

"What about cartridges?" Joshua asked, and the owner reached down, bringing up two boxes of .45s. Joshua began rotating the cylinders of one gun, filling each chamber with the deadly domes of lead, before starting on the second one.

"Better not load them up in here," the store owner cautioned. "One might go off accidentally." A weak smile came over his face that instantly disappeared when Joshua lifted both wheel guns. The store owner stared wide-eyed down twin barrels as the hammers clicked back.

"You believe in the Good Book?" Joshua asked, staring hard at the proprietor. He nodded, but was too thunderstruck to speak. "Good. It says the Lord giveth, and the Lord taketh away. We're here to do the taking part. Open up the cash box and dump it out on the counter."

Trey was so surprised at the sudden move that for a moment all he could do was stand and stare at his new partner. He had no choice but to carry through with the holdup, scooping up the money and filling his pockets. Then he ordered the owner into the back room, where they tied his hands and feet and gagged him, leaving him on the floor so they had time to clear out of town before he could free himself and yell for help. As they climbed back into their saddles and started down the street at a gallop, Trey looked over at Joshua.

"You sure you haven't done this before?"

Joshua smiled and shook his head. "Nope, only in my dreams. But I sure want to do a whole lot more of it!"

Trey warned him in no uncertain words not to try it again unless they planned something ahead of time. "You ride with me, you either do things my way or you can head back to Utah and your father, you understand? I don't want to get shot by accident."

The busy town of Nogales, Arizona, sat right on the border just yards away from another Nogales, this one in Mexico. When Trey and Joshua rode in weeks later, the first thing they noticed was the large number of Mexicans on the street. Neither had ever seen many before, sporting the big, round hats they called sombreros, shading dark faces adorned with black mustaches. A mixture of wooden buildings and tents lined the main street, harboring bars, assay offices, dry goods stores, and even a one-story wooden hotel for the few that could afford to stay there. Rented cots in the sleeping tents were far more popular and cheaper. Trey and Joshua chose to stay in a tent.

Business deals in trading, freighting, dry goods, and gold seemed to be going on everywhere. When the young guns walked into a big tent with the sign that said BAR out front, they got an ever bigger surprise. "How far is it to Mexico?" Trey asked the barman.

The barkeep smiled through his drooping handlebar mustache. "You must be new around here, huh?"

"What do you mean?" Trey shrugged.

"Just what I said. The dividing line between Arizona Territory and Sonora, Mexico, is right out there in the middle of the street. Once you cross it you're in Mexico. Now, are you two drinking or not?"

Trey ordered two whiskys, but Joshua admitted he'd never tasted the stuff before.

"You do it like this." Trey hooked the shot straight down, slamming the empty glass on the counter. "Go ahead," he urged, "you want to be a man, don't you?"

Joshua followed suit, pouring the amber-colored liquid straight down his throat. His face instantly turned red. He bent over, choking for breath, stamping his foot on the floor, as Trey slapped him on the back while laughing aloud. "You better stick to that Mormon lemonade, it's more your style. You leave the drinking to me."

The pair spent the rest of that day wandering around town, going in and out of stores and taking in busy Nogales. The gold mines just north of town fueled the community's existence and endless trading. They found it exciting. When they stopped on a corner late that afternoon after taking it all in, Trey had a sudden revelation.

"I just thought of something. Once we cross that street we're in Mexico, like the barkeep said. That means the law can't touch us over there. We're free as long as we stay there."

Joshua looked back with a growing smile. "Well, let's go to Mexico, then."

That evening they followed the sound of guitar music and singing into the Mexican Rose Cantina. The noisy, smoke-filled room was full of patrons as they edged their way over to a table and sat down. A fat Mexican in a dirty apron came over, greeting them in broken English. "Tequila, señors?"

"What's tequila?" Trey asked.

"Ahhhhh . . . like you Americano whid-skee. You savvy?" he said with a heavy accent.

"Mexican whisky, huh? Okay. Give us a couple of glasses." As the waiter headed for the bar, Trey looked around the room and realized they were the only Americans in the place.

Over in one corner, two Mexicans had been eyeing the pair since they walked in, especially the pearl-handled pistols Joshua had strapped on his hips. They leaned close, whispering to each other. When the counterman returned to Trey's table with their drinks, one of the Mexicans got to his feet and worked his way across the room. He came to a stop and stared down at the two Americans. A slow smile came over his pock-marked face as he leaned down, placing both hands on the table. "Amigos, do you mind if I sit for *uno momento*? I have a question for you."

Trey nodded toward the chair and the Mexican slid into it, leaning forward and talking in a low voice. "My amigo and I"—he glanced at his partner across the room—"are looking to hire *dos vaqueros* to ride with us. We haf a leetle job to do down south in our country. We need *pistoleros* not afraid to use their weapons. Are two looking for work?"

"We might be available depending on what kind of work you're talking about," Trey replied. The Mexican explained that he and his friend were hired as guards to take a gold shipment from one of the mines outside of town west to the coast and onto a ship for a trip south. The gold had to be transported two hundred miles to Guaymas by wagons. The long route would avoid the main road inland where bandits made it too risky to travel. Even some government shipments guarded by federal soldiers had been ambushed. The mining company devised the trip to the coast to avoid the chance of a loss.

"What's the pay?" Trey asked.

"De pay is one hundred American dollars each when we reach Guaymas. You two gringos look like you know how to handle your pistoleros, no?"

Trey glanced at Joshua, who smiled back and nodded slightly. "Okay. We'll hire on. You got yourself two gunnies. Now where and when do we meet you two for this little ride?"

The Mexican, who said his name was Santiago Mendes, told them he'd meet them there the following evening. He got to his feet and shook hands with both young guns as a slow smile lifted the thick, black mustache on his face.

"Looks like we got ourselves a job." Trey took a pull at the cloudy tequila swirling in his glass.

"Looks like." Joshua smiled the boyish grin of his.

After they left the cantina, the pair headed for the sleeping tent and cots they'd rented earlier that afternoon. The big tent held thirty canvas cots stacked so close together there was barely room to squeeze between them. For two bits, renters got one narrow cot, one thin blanket, one dirty pillow, and twelve hours to use it, depending on when you checked in with a man sitting at a desk at the flap entrance. His job was to collect the money, try to keep a marginal degree of order, and remove anyone who couldn't do either. A four-hole communal toilet was dug out back.

The tent reeked with the overpowering smell of humanity,

and the noise was deafening from the sound of snoring men. Grimy miners called it home, their sweat-soaked clothes and bodies permeating the heavy air. They were tough men. Day laborers bending their backs over picks and shovels, their lives strung together from one payday to the next and little thought of more. When payday came, most got roaring drunk, staggering back to their tent home where few got much sleep. Trey and Joshua were glad their stay would only last one more night, as they wound their way through the cots and then sat down.

"I'd almost go back to Utah than put up with this mess," Trey grumbled, pulling off his boots. "Tomorrow can't come soon enough for me."

"Not me," Joshua shot back. "I had all of that I want. Let's just try and get a little sleep. This ride to the coast sounds like a long one, and the law can't touch us once we start it." He unbuckled his gun belt, sliding it next to him under the blanket, as both men stretched out to try to get some rest.

Two hours later four drunk miners pushed the tent flap aside and staggered in, talking loudly as they bumped their way through cots and sleeping men. One, named Jack Hawkins, waved a half-empty whisky bottle. When he reached Trey's cot he stopped, weaving on his feet, looking down at the young man.

"Ain't this nice. School boys sleeping right in here with all us grown-up men." He leaned down closer. "Aww, he's sleeping like a baby. Maybe he needs a little drink too?"

Trey's eyes flickered open, staring up at the four faces until the images cleared. "Why don't you go to bed and shut up. You're bothering everyone, including me, whisky breath."

Jack Hawkins staggered back, fighting to keep his balance, as his pals laughed out loud. He leaned forward again, tipping his bottle down until a thin stream of alcohol dribbled onto

Trey's face, stinging his eyes like fire and temporarily blinding him. He kicked off the blanket. In a flash he was on his feet, his right hand smashing into the drunk's jaw and sending him reeling backward, crashing over cots and yelling men. His pals lifted him to his feet, blood streaming down his face from a broken nose. As he wiped it with one hand, the other pulled up a wicked-looking bowie knife, pushing off his friends as he lunged at Trey. Suddenly the air was shattered by three lightning fast pistol shots. Hawkins crumpled to the floor flat on his face while Joshua stood with his six-shooters smoking in his hands.

Now the tent came alive with yelling men diving under cots, while others grabbed up their goods and ran for the entrance, half-dressed and still half-asleep. Hawkins' pals backed up with their hands raised, wide-eyed with fear as Joshua swung dual sixes on them and ordered them to pick up their dead friend and get out.

Trey wiped the whisky from his face, turned to his young partner, and shook his head slightly. "You do like to pull a trigger, don't you?"

Joshua stared back, his sky blue eyes as cold as the death he'd just administered. That boyish grin came over his face again as he strapped on the holster snugging the .45s back in place. "Well, I had to save your bacon, didn't I? I sure don't want to make that long ride down to Mexico alone."

Chapter Eight

Rocky Road to Guaymas

 W ispy white clouds slowly swept the blue desert sky clean the next day, as Trey and Joshua passed the time by leaning back on their propped-up chairs against the Mexican Rose Cantina, watching a passing parade of people and riders.

"You know, I could get real used to doing nothing if it just paid a little better," Trey said, glancing over at the kid.

"I don't know about that, but I've always wanted to see the ocean. I've only read about it in books. Besides, a hundred dollars sounds real good too. Don't it to you?"

Trey admitted it did, but he had the feeling they were going to have to earn every penny of it. When Joshua asked why, he explained that Mendes could have hired any number of Mexicans to do exactly the same job they'd signed on for. Instead, he took two gringos, complete strangers. He wondered how just four guns could protect two wagons from bandit gangs if they ran into them. He warned that they'd be smart not only to keep their eyes on the gold, but Mendes and his pal tóo.

That evening at the Mexican Rose they met again with

70

Mendes and his silent partner. This time he introduced his friend as Carlos Monzone. Trey studied Monzone as Mendes continued talking. He noticed the man was older. His scarred face showed no sign of emotion, just the same blank stare from cold brown eyes. His hair was flecked with streaks of white, and his scraggly mustache was long and unkempt. But it was those milky white eyes Trey kept going back to. They said Monzone could kill at the drop of hat and think nothing of it.

Mendes told them to meet him the next day at the Luna Mine several miles outside of town, then finished with an admonition. "Carlos don spick de English too good. You jus talk to me, you savvy? I tell heem what you say, *comprendo?*"

The sun had barely cleared the hills when the young guns rode up to the Luna. Mendes and Monzone were already waiting for them, and the wagons were loaded as Mendes was engaged in animated conversation with the mine foreman. There seemed to be some kind of dispute going on between the two as the foreman continually gestured toward the two gringos. Finally, Mendes walked over to explain that the foreman thought they were too young and inexperienced to take on the job protecting the gold shipment. Trey glanced over at the boss and slowly eased out of the saddle, telling Joshua to fetch a tin can from the dump pile behind one of the shacks. He was back in a moment with one.

"Toss it out there on the ground." Trey nodded, his hands dropping to his side, just touching the smooth curve of his walnut pistol grips.

No sooner had it hit the dirt than Trey drew and fired, sending the vessel spinning into the air. The instant it hit the ground he fired again, the can darting away from a second bullet hit. When it landed again, Trey's wheel gun spoke for the third time, shredding what was left of it. He holstered his pistol while walking over to Mendes.

"Ask him if he thinks we're too young to protect the wagons now."

The foreman and Mendes had a brief conversation until Santiago came back. "Now we go. You two take de first wagon. Carlos and I weel follow wit de second one."

As the wagons lurched forward, rattling down the stony road away from the mine, the foreman stood with his hands on his hips studying the four riders. He still wasn't certain of his decision. Guaymas was still a long two hundred miles away. The gringo with the fast gun could shred tin cans, but was he that quick when someone was shooting back at him? Mendes and Monzone he knew from previous trips. These two gringos he still wasn't that sure about.

The rough road wound south, traversing brushy hills through stifling heat, and eventually passing the small roadside towns of Santa Ana and Querobabi until approaching Hermosillo, the biggest city on the route ninety miles from the coast, two weeks later. The riders were dusty, thirsty, and tired. They'd run into no trouble, but being constantly on edge expecting it had worn their nerves thin. Mendes decided the four should ride into town to take a break, get some decent food, and drink a little too. He ordered the wagoneers to stay outside of town and guard the gold while they were gone, promising they'd be back later that night.

Their first stop in Hermosillo was a small, side-street café where Mendes ordered food for all of them. He'd barely had time to light up his *cigaro* when steaming plates of tamales, beans, and rice were laid on the table. The four dug into the rich-tasting provender without paying any attention to the other customers curiously eyeing the two Americanos. This far below the border, gringos were rarely seen. After cleaning their plates, Mendes suggested they head for a cantina to have a drink before returning to the wagons.

Even after dark the narrow streets were crowded with people as they wound their way to the establishment until pushing through the front door. The place was alive with talk, blue smoke hanging over the room like a thick cloud, as the four headed for the bar. Men in big hats turned to stare at the odd foursome. Not all the looks were friendly.

News of skirmishes between the two countries along the border had been going on for years. Claims of the actual boundary line by the growing nation to the north caused even more tension and occasional gunfights. Gringos were not welcomed south of the border, although Trey and Joshua knew none of this.

For his part, the young ex-Mormon was having the time of his life. He'd escaped the domineering clutches of his father and the church. Now he had the kind of freedom he'd only dreamt of, and Trey had made it all possible. He never wanted the adventure to end. Although Trey never spoke about it openly, he knew the longer he stayed out of Wyoming, the better. A year, two years—what did it matter? He had to wait until things cooled down before even thinking about going back. Mexico seemed like a good place to do exactly that.

Mendes ordered a bottle of tequila. When the barkeep brought it over, the four headed for a table. None of them had noticed three uniformed federal police at the far end of the bar, who had been watching them from the moment they walked in. No sooner had they sat down and began pouring tequila than the *federales* started for them across the room.

Mendes was the first to notice them working their way between the tables. He turned to Trey. "Don meek no trouble. We have company. I do all dee talking, savvy?"

Trey looked up as the three policemen approached. They didn't wear a tin star, but their khaki uniforms and shoulder-strapped holsters were all he needed to see. Trey quickly kneed Joshua under the table. The look in Trey's eyes told Joshua all he needed to know, as both their hands went under the table, cradling their six-guns. The officers stopped at the table, staring first at the gringos, then at Mendes and Monzone. The conversation quickly became animated, and Trey didn't have to understand Spanish to know Mendes was not convincing the trio of anything. Finally, he turned back to Trey.

"Dees *policia* wan you to go weeth dem for questioning. Eet won't take long, I go weeth you."

"You tell them I'm not going anywhere. We're not bothering anyone in here. There's no reason for it. I'm not going to rot in some Mexican jail while they try and trump up some charge on either me or Joshua. Tell 'em what I said, and make it clear."

Mendes pulled at his jaw, eyes darting to Monzone before turning back to the officers to try to smooth out the answer. Before he could finish speaking, the lead officer's face fell and his eyes narrowed in anger. He said something to his partners, then reached for the pistol on his hip. He never cleared it.

"Take 'em, Joshua!" Trey yelled, and the pair kicked the table back, leaping to their feet with six-guns drawn, spitting fire and hot lead. The *federales* were driven back, crumpling to the floor by murderous, close-range fire as the room exploded in bedlam. Men dove under tables or jumped over the bar. For a fleeting second, even Mendes and his partner were so stunned they couldn't act. Then they came to their feet and grabbed the young guns, yelling at them to run for the door. Four shadowy figures sprinted down the darkened streets until they were lost in the evening crowd, while chaos reined back at the cantina.

When the four reached the wagon camp, Mendes kicked the drivers awake, shouting at them to get the horses harnessed quickly. The confused, half-awake pair tried to question him, but were ordered to do as they were told and not waste time. Mendes continued pushing them into action, then turned to Trey. "You keeled dos federal police officers! Do you know what dat means? De Army weel now come looking for us and shoot on sight!"

Trey leaned close, face-to-face with the Mexican. "I ain't letting no damn Mexican police or anyone else slap me in some stinking prison. You understand that, amigo? I'll kill anyone who tries it, Army or not. You wanted a couple of gun hands and now you've got 'em. You want to change that, pay us off and we'll clear out right now. You and Monzone can take the wagons ahead on your own. What's it going to be?"

Mendes glanced at his pal, who slowly shook his head no, then turned back to Trey. "Okay, gringo. We go to de coast. Den you and your friend go your own way. I do not wan to swing at the end of a rope weeth you two." He turned back to the wagon drivers. "*Vaminos*, amigos, pronto!"

The wagons rumbled down the road into the black of night while the twinkling lights of Hermosillo faded behind them.

Late the next afternoon, Mendes pointed to a low grove of trees and ordered the drivers to pull over and stop for the day. Trey looked over his shoulder. The road was empty, with no sign of distant dust rising.

"There's no one following us," he said to Santiago. "Why don't we keep on going at least until dark?"

Art Isberg

"No." Mendes shook his head. "*Des caballos* need rest for a leetle while. Maybe den we move on. Not now."

Trey glanced at Joshua. He didn't know why they were stopping. The look on his face said it all. After tying the horses off, Trey got down to talk to Joshua off to one side. "Keep your eyes open. Stopping here doesn't make any sense. If these two greasers try something, we better be ready for it."

They watched as Mendes and Monzone walked past the wagons, climbing a low hill just back of the trees. They stood there, hands raised to their eyes to shield them from the sun. After a few minutes of looking off to the north, Monzone walked back down the hill and passed Trey. He decided to try something he'd thought about before. "Did you see anything out there?" he asked.

Monzone answered no, shaking his head.

"I thought you couldn't understand any English. You understood that plain enough," Trey challenged him.

The Mexican glared back, caught in his own lie, and turned away for the wagons without answering.

Trey looked back up the hill. Mendes was still up there, staring off someplace. He hadn't moved an inch. What was he looking for? Trey wondered. There had to be someone out there. Why else would they stop here at this odd time of day? He finally decided it was time he found out for himself.

"You keep your eyes on Monzone," he said to Joshua. "I'm going up there to get some answers out of Mendes if possible."

He stepped out of the shade of the trees and started up the hill, the desert sun white hot on his back. He lifted his six-gun, slightly loosening it in its holster, for a quick pull if need be. As he approached, Mendes turned, surprised to see Trey instead of Monzone. Before he could say a word, Trey spoke up.

"What are you looking for up here? Who are you waiting for?" he asked, coming face-to-face with Mendes.

"No-ting," the Mexican answered. But Wingo knew the sweat running down Mendes' face came from more than just afternoon heat. He continued to deny Trey's assertions and, as Trey badgered him further, looked past him until the images of three riders came into view on the horizon through dancing waves of heat.

"What about them?" He nodded. "I suppose you don't know anything about that either, huh?"

Mendes turned, squinting at the trio coming closer. He took off his big hat, wiping his face with his shirtsleeve. As he put the hat back on, his other hand went down for his pistol and he spun to face Trey. But Trey was quicker. Two fast shots rang out at point-blank range, and Mendes went rolling down in the sand. In the same instant, Trey heard gunfire erupt from the wagon camp as Monzone and Joshua traded pistol shots, and the pair of unarmed drivers ran for cover.

Trey took one quick look at the riders coming closer and then sprinted downhill, six-gun in hand. Coming around the back of one wagon, he caught Monzone in a murderous cross-fire.

The Mexican spun while firing at Trey, wagon sideboards splintering from bullet hits that missed. The gringo emptied his gun into Monzone, who sagged to the ground, dropping his pistol. Both hands covered the bullet holes in his belly until he rolled over facedown in the sand and stopped moving.

When Joshua ran up, Trey quickly told him about the riders coming in. "Quick, let's get the rifles. We're going to need them. It looks like Mendes meant to ambush us right here and take the wagons until his friends showed up. They've probably been trailing us since we left Hermosillo. Now we've got to deal with them too."

They ran for their rifles and returned to take cover behind a wagon, waiting for the riders to come in. Five minutes passed, then ten, fifteen, and still no one showed. Joshua whistled to Trey, but all he could was shrug. Had the horsemen heard the shooting and turned back? Trey straightened up and peered over the sideboards, looking up on the hilltop, still waiting for them to show. Suddenly shots rang out from the edge of the trees to his right, then left. The riders had dismounted and snuck around the edge of the hill to try to catch the young guns by surprise.

They both leaped up into the wagons, using the ore boxes for protection and firing back at blue puffs of smoke erupting from cover. Rifles continued barking as bullets ricocheted off the heavy cargo and the battle raged on, but neither Trey nor Joshua could score a hit on the well-entrenched trio. That's when Joshua leapt from the wagon on a daring run, dodging bullets kicking up at his heels as he ran for a rocky spur where one bandito was firing from. When the frantic Mexican emptied his rifle and was trying to reload, Joshua dashed straight for him until clearing the stony fortress, firing as the wide-eyed man threw both hands up to cover himself. It was the last thing he ever saw as rifle fire exploded in his face.

As suddenly as it began, the firing stopped. Trey could hear one of the Mexicans yelling up on the hill. A minute later, he heard the sound of horses' hooves thundering away, fading fast. He got to his feet and ran up the sandy slope until he stood on top. He saw a pair of riders streaking away over the hills. He waved an all clear to Joshua and started back down the hill.

At the wagons they stripped Monzone of his gun belt and cartridges. Already the drone of flies grew in volume as the smell of death permeated the hot, late-afternoon air, and they settled on the body. Trey called the drivers back from hiding, ordering them to get back up on the reins, as Joshua cocked his head with a question.

"What are we going to do now?"

"We're going on to Guaymas, just like we started out to do. You said you wanted to see the ocean, didn't you? Besides, we've still got money to collect for delivering these wagons."

Joshua smiled and nodded his head as he reloaded his rifle. Trey never ceased to amaze him. And that killing afternoon on the road to the coast was just another example of why.

Chapter Nine

Cortez Blue

For the next four weeks, the young guns pushed the wagons relentlessly until finally coming through the last stony mountains surrounding the sprawling town of Guaymas, fronting the Sea of Cortez. That late afternoon the air was blistering hot and dead still, the ocean calm as the wagon drivers, who had made this trip before, pulled to a stop at a long wooden pier leading out into deeper water. At the far end, a small, single-stack freighter slowly rose and fell on gentle swells.

Joshua eased out of the saddle, pushing his hat back on his head and shielding his eyes from the dazzling reflection of sun off water, as gentle waves hissed up on white sands then retreated. He looked over at Trey, shaking his head at the amazing sight.

"Well, you wanted to see the ocean. Here it is." Trey leaned forward on the saddle horn, his eyes following the pier out to the cargo ship then back to his sidekick.

Joshua knelt at the waters edge, putting both hands into the cool surf. It felt so refreshing after weeks of fighting the smothering heat of the interior that he washed his face and then licked his lips. "It's salty," he called out, and Trey smiled back.

"I'd guess most oceans are. Let's get these wagons unloaded. That's what that ship out there must be waiting for."

The wagon drivers, who spoke no English, pointed toward the vessel, nodding their heads as Trey led the way out over the wooden planks and the freighters rumbled after him. As they approached, Trey's eyes wandered over its dilapidated superstructure. Any vestige of paint had long since peeled away. Its wooden sides were dented and splintered from years of use, and up in the wheelhouse the windows were so dirty he could barely make out the figure of a man standing behind the glass. Four deckhands moved to the rail as Trey got down.

"Anyone here speak English?" He looked from one brown face to another but didn't get a response.

"No comprenda," one man finally spoke up, shrugging, as his pals stared back at the two gringos.

"I speak English!" A voice boomed out from the elevated steel platform surrounding the wheelhouse, as Trey and Joshua looked up to see a big man wearing a tattered captain's hat, with curly gray muttonchops that ran down to his jaw and the stump of a black twist cigaro sticking out the side of his mouth. "Where's Mendes and Mozone? That's who I usually pick up here."

"They couldn't make it," Trey shot back. "Me and my partner came instead."

The big man eyed them a moment longer before speaking again. "Name's Quinn. Loyal Quinn. This here is my ship, the *Dorado*. Let's get that ore loaded onboard before the tide ebbs. We can be in blue water before sundown, and Porto Oro by dawn."

"What about our horses?" Trey questioned.

"Load them too." Quinn turned to his deckhands, shouting orders as the four scrambled to drop the sideboards and led the first wagon onto the little freighter. They positioned the wagon while two men held the horses steady. The other pair opened a hatch hole in the deck, then went to the back of the wagon, pulling the tailgate down. The stony rumble of heavy ore falling into the cargo hold started the horses jittering around as the drivers got down and held them too. When the ore stopped falling, the deckhands grabbed shovels and jumped up into the wagon, continuing to clean it out by hand. In forty minutes the first wagon was empty, led back onto the dock, and the second brought on.

When it was emptied, Quinn called Trey and Joshua up to the wheelhouse deck. Trey climbed the ladder, but Joshua walked to the bow, gripping the iron railing and staring out at the glittering sundown on the Cortez Sea. He was transfixed by the sight of it.

Mooring lines were thrown off. The stack belched a cloud of black smoke, and down in the bowels of the vessel the engine shuddered to life and slowly began moving away from the dock.

Joshua continued to stare down into the water almost hypnotized, watching it turn from mottled tan to dark green, and eventually deep blue. Up in the wheelhouse, Quinn gripped the big wooden wheel with both hands while staring out the window as Guaymas grew smaller behind them. He glanced over at Trey, wondering what a young man like him was doing way down here in Mexico running ore wagons to the coast. He decided he'd try and find out.

"Don't see many Americans this far south of the border." He pursed his thick lips. "Except for hauling some prospectors over to Yucatán, you're the first ones I've seen in about six months."

Trey admitted they hadn't planned to end up in Mexico until they got the job offer back in Nogales. "Why are they hauling all this ore by ship?" he asked Quinn.

The captain explained that gold and silver strikes across the Sea of Cortez on the Yucatán peninsula had concentrated mining activity there as well as the building of ore smelters. The robberies and murders on the mainland roads had led many mining companies to avoid that route and instead cross the waters to Yucatán, processing their ore there. "What are they paying you and your friend out there for bringing the wagons down?"

When Trey told him one hundred dollars apiece, Quinn scoffed. "Ha! For a hundred dollars I wouldn't take them wagons ten miles. They got you two cheap. You're lucky you didn't have to go up against any road gangs. What they should'a paid you is about five hundred each for this kind of work. I see your friend out there likes them fancy guns of his. Does he know how to use them?"

Trey admitted Joshua came in pretty handy at times, and not to let his schoolboy looks fool him. He walked to the window and stared down at Joshua. His thoughts flashed back to Utah and how much he'd begrudged taking the Mormon with him. Then he thought about Johnny. Was he still there on the Logan ranch, still lovestruck over Laura Logan, or had he taken her, as he said he would, back to Montana to turn himself in? If Johnny could only see him now, he wouldn't believe where he was or what he was doing, riding the deep blue swells of the Cortez on a rickety old freighter. He almost couldn't believe it himself, the way everything had happened. Then Quinn's voice in the background broke his daydreaming.

"We should make port by morning. If you two want to get some sleep, there's bunks down past the galley."

Trey stepped out of the wheelhouse door and went down the ladder onto the deck. Up front Joshua was still staring out into the darkness. Trey came up behind him, shaking him by the shoulder, and suggested they try to get a little shut-eye. The kid turned and nodded, as Trey led the way through a door under the wheelhouse down past the galley into a darkened room.

The stifling air reeked with the smell of dirty clothes and sweat-stained bodies and the sound of snoring men. A pair of rope-hung hammocks swayed back and forth to the rhythm of the ship. Trey pulled himself up into the first one, then Joshua did the same.

For a long time both men lay there staring up into the dark. The throbbing engine in the next compartment came right through the bulkhead and pounded in their ears. Trey twisted, pulling his hat down over his head, trying to drown out the incessant racket, but he couldn't. A short time later he felt someone pulling at his arm. It was Joshua. "Let's go up on deck. At least it's cool, and the stink stays down here."

Back out under the stars, they spread saddle blankets and lay down. The cool night air felt refreshing, and the gentle tempo of the swells finally brought some relief from the misery down below. Just before Trey fell asleep, he looked up at the dim glow of light from the wheelhouse. Quinn was still there, at the wheel, staring off into the night.

When Trey awoke, the rising sun was painting his face, and the shrill cry of seagulls soared over his head. He lay there a moment longer studying the graceful birds as they floated back and forth with barely a pump of their wings. Their yellow beaks and creamy white bodies were tinged in gold from the new sun. He rolled up on one elbow, taking in the blue Cortez. He was able to make out the silhouette of low, tan hills on the horizon. He sat up, rubbed the sleep out of his eyes, and shook Joshua awake.

"Look out there." He pointed. "That must be Yucatán. We'd better get up."

Quinn slid the wheelhouse window open and pulled the boat whistle, announcing to shore they were getting close. One by one small figures appeared on the dock as his own hands came up the ladder, disheveled and still half-asleep, until his sharp voice roused them to prepare for unloading.

The young guns went to the bow, watching the land come closer, studying the dry, barren hills that ran right down to the water's edge. A scattering of low shacks dotted the shoreline, and out on the dock itself, a crane hung motionless, its steel bucket empty, waiting to unload their stony cargo. As they came in Quinn throttled back the engine, creeping slowly closer until coming alongside the dock with just the slightest bump, and two deckhands stepped out to secure the ship fore and aft with thick hawsers.

"You two get your horses off first!" he yelled from the wheel-house. "Once they start unloading the oar, they won't like the racket. Tie 'em off by that tin shed up there at the end of the dock. That's the pay station. I'll be up there when we're done. They don't speak no American, so you'll have to wait for me, but it wouldn't be a bad idea if you two tried to learn some of their lingo. You're gonna need it if you plan on staying down here for very long."

The morning sun rose and, with it, the building heat. Two hours later the ship was unloaded, and Quinn trudged up to the shack, sweat pouring down his whiskered face. "Okay, let's go inside and get us some *dinero*. They owe me too, not just you two." He smiled, a fresh cigaro in his mouth.

Inside the little building, Quinn greeted the paymaster with a handshake, as the rotund Mexican eyed his two friends. He said something to Quinn and grinned, as he nodded toward Trey and Joshua, then turned and knelt to a wheel safe over in one corner.

"Domingo wants to know if I've thrown in with two gunmen, because of all that iron you're packing on your hips." Quinn laughed under his breath.

The manager came back to the counter, placing a metal box on top and opening the lid. He carefully thumbed through a stack of bills, counted three smaller ones, and pushed them across.

"This is Mexican money. I can't use that. Tell him to pay us in American," Trey complained.

Quinn turned to him with a slow smile. "This is it, boy. You're in Mexico now, remember? There ain't no American money down here except maybe in banks. You better learn how to spend it. Let's go up to what these wharf rats call a cantina, and I'll explain it to you."

They went back outside up the hill past a row of tin-roofed shacks with little children standing at the doors, wide-eyed while watching the strange gringos pass. Quinn nodded to a larger building with faded writing over the entrance, stepping into the shadowed interior. It took a few moments for their eyes to adjust from glaring sunlight. When they did, Trey and Joshua looked around a dingy room with half a dozen men sitting at tables scattered over a dirt floor, staring back at them. Quinn stepped up to the bar and ordered three bottles of beer.

"This round's on me." He grabbed the bottles and headed for an empty table. "Next one's on you two. You call this beer, but down here it's called *cerveza*. Start learning that right now."

He lifted his bottle in a toast. "Here's to the good ol' U.S. of A. May it always stay north of the border!"

After washing the dust and heat from their throats, Quinn pulled out his wallet and placed three different denominations of bills on the table, explaining what each one was worth. After half a dozen empty bottles lined the table, Trey thought he understood the difference. The captain asked him what he and his sidekick were going to do now, ride back to Guaymas with him or stay on the peninsula for a while.

"If you decide to stay, both of you should ride down to La Paz or Cabo San Lucas. Maybe even San Jose del Cabo. There's lots to see, including some pretty señoritas."

They finished their cerveza and walked back down to the dock. Quinn stuck out his hand. "If I was thirty years younger I just might be tempted to sell the *Dorado* and ride down south with you two. I guess now I've got too much of the Cortez in my blood. Remember what I said. You're not north of the border anymore. Things are different down here. So are the people. You'll have to get used to that. Look me up when you come back if you want to go to the mainland. I'll still be around. Good luck, gringos!"

They watched the big man saunter down to his vessel. He climbed aboard, turning once to wave before starting up the ladder to the wheelhouse. Joshua looked at Trey. "Well, I'm in no rush to leave the Yucatán, are you?"

Trey glanced at his young apprentice with that wicked smile of his. "Nope. Let's go see La Paz!"

Chapter Ten

La Paz

The long, hot coastal road south to La Paz wound through dry, rocky mountains rimmed with white sand beaches and scattered fishing villages washed by the deep, blue Sea of Cortez. Five days after leaving Porto Oro, Trey and Joshua reined to a stop overlooking the big fishhook-shaped bay fronting the city itself. The wide spread of multicolored huts and houses running back from the water showed La Paz to be the biggest town they'd seen since leaving Hermosillo on the mainland.

Joshua leaned forward on his saddle horn to view the panorama while taking off his hat and wiping the sweat from his face with the back of his shirtsleeve. "You know what I need most right now?" he asked as he turned to Trey.

"No, what?"

"Some shade, a cool drink of water, and a good bath. Doesn't Mexico ever have a rainy day or some winter sometime? This heat would fry a rattlesnake."

"Look way out there." Trey pointed to a thin curtain of gray showers moving slowly across the sea toward the town. "There's your rain, but I'd agree we both could use a rest. So can these horses. Let's ride into town and see where we can stay."

Trey didn't say so out loud, but the long ride was more than just a sightseeing trip. He knew they needed a big town with lots of people and businesses plus the money that kept them alive. Mexico was in the throes of a serious upheaval. The largely poor working class had grown weary of government corruption at all levels. The politicians and rich lived extravagantly, while the masses barely eked out a living. Trey had noticed this ever since they crossed the border back in Nogales, and it meant that the lack of law would offer him and Joshua the chance to profit at what they did best.

North of the border, lawmen would chase you down for weeks, sometimes months, riding hundreds of miles to do so if they had to. Not here. Not in Mexico. The country was wide open and ripe for profit for the man with a quick gun and a fast horse. La Paz should be the perfect setting to carry it out.

As they rode down the beach toward town, Trey noticed another small fishing village tucked away in a side canyon just off the beach. Brightly colored boats were pulled up on the sand, their nets hung out to dry in the hot sun and warm wind off the ocean. He pulled to a stop, studying the shacks built on stilts, then motioned Joshua to follow him, kicking his horse closer until he stopped in front of one with an old Mexican sitting on his heels.

"Howdy." He tipped his hat, but the old man just stared back as Trey eyed the line of huts. "You got any of these for rent?" He tried again and got the same result until Joshua reached in his pocket and pulled out a wad of bills with one hand, pointing at the shacks with the other. The old man's eyes widened, and a toothless grin spread across his face as he got to his feet and motioned for them to follow him.

He led them up the draw to the last hut at the far end, climbing rickety stairs to push aside a woven mat that served as the front door. Inside, the uneven bamboo walls allowed the sea breeze to waft through the structure, and its palm-thatched roof did the same. Except for the constant smell of fish from the other huts, the place seemed ideal to Trey. It was out of town, isolated, and unnoticed. A pair of gringos could retreat to it if things got too tight.

"Okay, we'll take it." Trey held out some bills. The old man pulled three off the top, handing the roll back and nodding with a smile.

"What did we just pay for rent? A day, week, or month?" Joshua wondered out loud.

"Beats me. But when he comes back for more I guess we'll find out then, huh?"

Over the next two months the pair explored the many streets and alleys comprising the sprawling city of La Paz. They began to learn the best curbside eating carts and restaurants with their rich provender of tamales, tortillas, beans, rice, and chicken dishes. At night they frequented cantinas where music blared and tequila and mescal flowed freely in smoke-filled rooms. Two months turned to four, then six. Life was good.

At one cantina, Casa Ramos, a pretty young Mexican girl named Chita Ovalis sang and danced every night to the sound of guitar music. She was a favorite of customers as she twirled through the crowded room taunting drinkers with a fake kiss, a shake of her low-cut blouse, and wicked wiggle when she danced away to the next man, hands on her hips, a bright, red rose pinned behind her ear. Joshua exclaimed he thought she was the prettiest girl he'd ever seen. Trey just sat and stared at her when she danced by.

She noticed the two young Americans the very first night they came in. Gringos were a rare sight in La Paz. On the mainland, that might be different, but out across the Cortez it was unusual. Even more noticeable to her were their ages. She was certain they were only a few years older than she. They were not the leering old men she was used to pretending to entice. Trey, especially, caught her eye. His tall build, good looks, and cool demeanor made her wonder what he was doing this far south of the border. When she danced close to his table, he never tried to reach out and grab her like everyone else or entice her to sit down with a drink. He just sat with that slow smile of his staring back. One night she decided to find out more about this strange young gringo after she finished her songs.

As the musicians wandered the room singing, she came through the tables where Trey and Joshua were sitting, smiling down on them with hands on her curvy hips. "Are you going to invite me to seet down?" she asked. Trey got to his feet and pulled out a chair for her. "I don't see many Americanos here before. You stay long een La Paz?"

Trey explained they didn't know how long they would call La Paz home, that they were just traveling, looking the country over. He added how surprised he was she could speak some English.

"I learn a leetle beet from my *madre*." Her gaze stayed fixed on Trey. "She learn from a gringo she once live weeth. Do you two live here in La Paz?"

Trey told her that they had a small place north of town out on the beach. As the conversation continued, Joshua could see her interest was fixed on his sidekick, for she rarely took her eyes off him. Finally, he pushed his chair back, telling them he was heading home to turn in. Chita glanced up at him with a short good-bye and turned back to Trey.

As the night went on they shared shots from a bottle of tequila until it stood nearly empty on the table. She showed him how to suck a lemon then lick salt off the back of his hand before drinking, until her hand moved to touch and squeeze his as they both told stories about themselves until after midnight. Suddenly, she changed the conversation. "Are you hungry, Trey?" she asked.

He smiled back at her, their eyes locked on each other, and he nodded slowly. "Yeah, I could use something to eat. Where do you want to go?"

She got to her feet without saying another word, pulling him up with her as they exited Casa Ramos. Out on the deserted street she led him down one darkened alley after another until he was completely lost, finally stopping at stairs leading up to an apartment. At the top she inserted a key into the lock, and they stepped inside a darkened room. Trey waited for her to light a candle, but instead he felt her hot breath on his face as her hands encircled his head, pulling him down and kissing him hard on the lips, while her hands caressed his neck. She tasted sweet, like tequila and lipstick, warm and delicious.

They clung to each other until both ran out of breath, and he swept her up in his arms as she cradled her head on his chest, kissing his neck. "Where do I sleep?" His voice was low, barely a whisper. She pointed into the living room, and he felt his way through the dark, stopping at a couch. "You mean here?"

"Yes, this is where you sleep. We are just friends now, Trey. And for now that's the way I want to keep it until I'm sure of other things. Do you understand what I'm saying?"

"Yes, I guess I do, but I thought maybe we were more than that, the way you've been looking at me each night at the cantina."

When Trey awoke in the morning, bright sunlight was streaming into the room from a big open window next to the couch. He glanced at the azure sky outside, then heard the faint sounds of people talking down on the street below. He turned back to stare at the bedroom door. This young Mexican woman had his head spinning. Just when he thought he had her figured out, she turned out to be exactly the opposite, making him dead wrong. But for this one moment in time he almost felt free, unwanted by the law, something close to the normal life he'd once known so far away to the north before he ever pulled a trigger in anger.

It was too good to last, and he knew that. Yet he couldn't help but revel in the pleasure at least for these brief few hours. Trey laid back on the couch staring at the ceiling, wondering how things had ever gotten this crazy. La Paz and Chita Ovalis could suddenly become something too special, too hard to break away from, too dangerous for a young desperado on the run. Just as bad, he wasn't exactly sure what to do about it.

When he rode back to the beach village later that afternoon, Joshua was sitting in front of their platform shack with a bottle of beer in his hand, relaxing. He shielded his eyes as Trey came down, climbing the steps. "Sleep good, did you?" Joshua asked, smiling.

"Yeah, I slept all right."

"I hope one night in town doesn't mean I've lost my roommate."

"Nah, not like that. We still have to watch each other's back. That won't change. But a little break every once in a while don't hurt either, you know?"

"I guess not. But you know our cash is beginning to run sort of low. We're going to have to do something pretty quick." Joshua got to his feet, running his hands through his hair with a more serious look.

"I know. But right now I want to kick out of these boots and go down to feel some cool water on my feet. We'll worry about the money later."

Several nights later, the young guns were back at Casa Ramos, watching Chita, when two men started through the crowd toward their table. As they came close, Trey nudged Joshua under the table to hint that they were about to have company. They were more surprised to see the pair were Americans, the only ones they'd seen since leaving Quinn back in Porto Oro. The two stopped, the taller man leaning down to introduce himself.

"Name's Jack Cain." He stuck out a hand. "This here is my partner, Luke Estees. You two mind if we sit down? You're the first Americans we've seen since we got here six months ago."

Trey nodded to the empty chairs, and the pair slid into them. Jack was slender, in his mid-forties, and did all the talking. The older Luke just sat back staring at Trey and Joshua. Without actually admitting it, Jack inferred they were both in Mexico to avoid a "rope party" back in the States. He wondered if Trey and Joshua might not be in the same boat, but Trey didn't give him a hint of why they were in La Paz. After a few rounds of drinks, Jack suggested that four Americans who found themselves south of the border and short of funds might want to consider a way to become solvent again. Trey glanced at Joshua then Jack for a moment without saying a word. He straightened up in his chair, leaning slightly forward. "So, how would you do that?" he questioned with a fixed stare.

Jack explained that the Mexican federal police garrisoned in La Paz was paid from the mainland by boat out of Mazatlan across the Sea of Cortez, where gold and silver mines had been hugely profitable. The boat docked at Cabo San Lucas first, to pay local city employees, then was brought north to

La Paz by wagon generally guarded by no more than three or four *federales*.

"It would be easy pickin's done right," Jack insisted. "We can take the wagon halfway up here on the road. It's never been robbed, and no one thinks it ever will be. Once we disarm the guards we can clean it out, unhitch the horses, and run them off so everyone is afoot, and then ride back here and get lost in the crowd before they can even sound an alarm. Luke and I have thought it through a dozen times. It'll work just like I said." He looked to Trey, then Joshua for some sign of interest.

"Lost in the crowd, huh?" Trey finally spoke up. "We're all Americans, and the only ones in the whole damn town. How long do you think it will take before they figure out who took the payroll?"

This time Luke spoke up. "We've thought of that too. We buy all Mexican clothes—pants, jackets, big hats. If we wear bandanas over our faces, they'll never know the difference. No one will be able to identify us. Pretty good, huh?"

Trey leaned back in the chair, thinking it over. He still wasn't sure it was all that simple, even though the plan did sound possible. "Tell you what," he answered, "we'll think on it first. When does this pay wagon show up?"

"Next week, usually on Tuesday, if they don't hit rough water out on the Cortez," Jack answered.

"We'll meet you back here in two days with a yes or no." Trey nodded as the four shook hands all around. Jack and Luke got to their feet and moved off into the room.

Chapter Eleven

Road Kill

At closing time later that night Trey and Chita headed for her apartment, while Joshua rode back to the village alone. She fixed them something to eat while Trey stayed quiet, thinking about Jack's proposition. After eating, they had a few drinks then went to bed in the wee hours of the morning. Trey lay stretched out on his stomach as Chita slowly massaged his back, her small, firm hands trying to relax his taught muscles.

"Why are you so quiet tonight?" she asked, pulling him closer and kissing him gently on the neck. "Ess someting wrong?"

He rolled over, looking into her big, dark eyes, kissing her lightly on the lips. He explained that he was going to be gone for a few days and to not worry about it.

"Where you go?"

"Just out of town. It's not important, so don't ask."

She pouted and rolled away from him, but he wrapped his strong arms around her as she pretended to struggle, until giving in and turning back to kiss him long and hard on the lips.

"Are all gringos like you? Dey don't say nothing that ees in de heart?"

"I don't know about all gringos. Only me. And no, I don't say what's in my heart because tomorrow it could all end. Now kiss me and don't ask me any more questions, okay? Let's enjoy what time we have and not worry about tomorrow."

When the four Americans met again, Trey said he and Joshua were in on the holdup. The next day they purchased the clothes and hats, then left town riding south down the road toward Cabo San Lucas. Late that night they made camp, waiting for tomorrow and the pay wagon.

As they sat around a small campfire eating tortillas, Trey looked across the flickering flames at his new partners. He figured Jack was pretty much what you saw. Tall, mild-mannered, he could have easily been a gentleman rancher, yet here he was south of the border planning robberies and living off the proceeds. Luke was a different breed. Cold and hawklike, he rarely cracked a smile, never letting anyone know what he was really thinking. He was older than Jack, and Trey figured he'd spent his entire life on the wrong side of the law thieving, robbing, and probably even murdering. Trey didn't trust him, and he made a mental note to tell Joshua not to either.

"What time does this pay wagon show up?" Joshua broke the silence.

"About middle morning, if the boat's on time," Jack answered. "Me and Luke also thought it might be a smart idea if he rode out tomorrow morning about five miles down the road and let us know when it comes in sight. Then we can set up for it."

Trey said that made sense and the four finished eating, put

out the fire, then rolled up in their blankets. Trey slid his six-gun under the saddle blanket he was using for a pillow.

Dawn was a tequila glow when Joshua rolled over in his blanket whispering to Trey next to him. "You awake?"

"I . . . am . . . now." Trey turned over, lifting off the blanket and sitting up.

"You trust those two?" Joshua nodded toward Jack and Luke, still asleep.

"We have to, but keep your eyes on Estees. I'm not so sure about him."

As the sun rose the four men got up, ate the remainder of last night's dinner, and discussed the wagon's schedule. Two hours later Luke mounted up and started down the road south to watch for the wagon's arrival. Trey suggested they take up positions on a high point where the wagon would have to slow down in order to make a steep climb before leveling out. Jack and Luke would take one side of the road, he and Joshua the other. They spread out, waiting.

The Yucatán sun rose higher until shimmering heat waves turned the hard pan road into a dancing snake as far as the eye could see. Jack checked his watch. A quarter to ten.

Luke should have been back by now. He wondered where he was. He took off his hat, wiping the growing sweat from his brow, then checked his pistol for the third time. He looked across the road to Trey and Joshua crouched behind a rock pile, shrugging about the time.

Ten o'clock came and went. Ten-twenty and then ten-thirty passed. Still Luke didn't show. The three men finally stood to stretch out the kinks, looking off to the south. Jack walked to the edge of the hill and squinted, shielding his eyes with both hands. He thought he saw a distant plume of dust. Five minutes later he was sure of it. It had to be Luke. He ran back, waving to Trey and Joshua.

Luke rode in, leaping down from his horse. "The wagon is about five miles back, but they've got *eight* federales riding with it, instead of four!"

"Eight!" Jack's voice was tight with concern. "You certain?"

"I counted every damn one of 'em twice. Maybe they're replacements for the garrison, but they're with 'em, all right. You still think we ought to try for it with that many?"

Jack turned to look at Trey and Joshua. The uncertainty on his face was obvious. He rubbed the back of his neck, slowly shaking his head. "I don't know about trying to take on eight."

Trey put both hands on his hips, staring back down the road. Dead silence hung in the air for several seconds before he questioned Luke. "Is the driver armed too?"

Luke said he had a sidearm, but his hands were full handling the four-horse team.

"Then I say we still take it. We're here, and we all need the money. We can take the wagon right at the top of hill. You and Jack take one side of the road, Joshua and I the other. If we can catch them from both sides we might be able to disarm them before they know what hit them."

"What if they put up a fight?" Jack questioned.

"Then it's two men apiece for each of us, and you'd better shoot fast and straight. Now let's get set up."

The blurry image of wagon and riders slowly began to take shape as the pay wagon rumbled closer, and the four highwaymen peeked from their boulder-strewn hideouts, watching it come closer. Joshua's hands went down, and he lifted both pearl-handled six-guns from their holsters, pulling both hammers back to full cock. He glanced at Trey. His eyes were narrow slits locked on the approaching wagon, studying the position of the escorts as sweat ran down his face from under the big sombrero he was wearing. Trey looked across the road to their partners. Jack lifted a hand signaling they were ready too. The wagon reached the bottom of the hill and started up toward them. Trey leaned lower, still as a rattler ready to strike. The wagon came closer.

The rattle of the wagon over stony ground grew louder as it climbed closer. The driver's command to the straining horses could be heard over the crack of his whip. A uniformed captain was in the lead, twisting in the saddle and yelling something at the driver. Four pairs of gringo eyes riveted on him. His six subordinates were mounted two by two behind him. The wagon began to slow as it neared the top of the grade, the whip lashing out again and again, driving the team toward its final goal. Trey got his feet under him, hissing to Joshua, "Now!"

Four figures leaped from cover, dashing for the road only yards away. "Get your hands up, and get down from those horses!" Trey gestured to the stunned captain, eyes wide, slowly lifting his hands. Even though he didn't understand a word of English, he understood five pistol barrels leveled on him and his men. Trey motioned for him to get down as Jack and Luke moved among the escorts, gesturing for them to do the same, pronto.

"Get their guns!" Trey shouted. "Toss them off into the rocks. Joshua, get that driver down out of that wagon now!"

Joshua moved toward the wagon as Jack and Luke lined the *federales* up alongside the road with their hands up. As Joshua approached the driver, he let the reins fall from his hands, suddenly diving for a shotgun kept in front of the seat. He started to yell a warning, but too late, as the whip man came up with the scattergun, pulling off both barrels in the same instant

Joshua's six-guns spit flame and lead in rapid succession, the driver crashing facedown on the floorboards.

The sudden explosion of shooting sent the horses wildly bolting away. Jack and Luke spun from guarding the troops to see Trey rolling on the ground, grimacing in pain and grabbing at both legs, which had been hit by a load of double-ought buckshot. The captain saw his chance, bolting and shouting at his men to flee as he frantically dove for his weapon among the rocks and brush. Luke turned back, firing at the scattering troops as the officer came up firing his pistol. Jack instantly went down, a bullet in his back, as all hell broke loose.

Joshua opened fire at the fleeing troops running downhill, as Trey, still on the ground, rolled over, firing at the officer just yards away. The captain cried out in pain as his pistol spun from his hands and he rolled over, wounded, pulling himself up into a ball.

"Let them go!" Trey shouted. "Get me up on my feet and get that payroll money from the wagon!"

Joshua ran to lift Trey, his pant legs already spreading with red blossoms from buckshot hits. He dragged him to the sideboards of the wagon as Trey hung on, and Joshua ran around the back, dropping the tailgate and pulling the canvas cover back. He lifted out two metal boxes, shooting the locks off the lids, as Luke ran up wide-eyed in fear. "Jack ain't gonna make it. He's paralyzed, can't move, and you're about shot to pieces too, Wingo!"

Trey braced himself upright, ordering Luke to shut up and bring the horses over. The coins were poured into three saddlebags as Trey gripped the saddle horn of his horse for support, leaning against it while slowly staggering over to where Jack lay faceup, quivering in death. Jack blinked as Trey came over and stared down at him.

"I—I—don't think I can get on my—horse." Jack barely got the words out.

"You're right," Trey nodded, grimacing in pain, "and we can't leave you here for the Mexicans to find either. Even if you lived, they'd torture you until you told them what they wanted to know. I can't let that happen, Jack. You have to understand that."

Jack's eyes followed Trey's hand as it moved down to his six-gun, pulled it out of its holster, and cocked the hammer full back, leaving him staring down the black hole of the barrel. He tried to lift his hands over his face before the pistol shot exploded straight down but didn't make it. Luke ran up, incredulous at the sudden execution.

"What in hell are you doing!" he screamed.

"I don't have time to explain it. Get on your horse and let's get out of here. Joshua, help me up into the saddle!"

As Joshua lifted his partner, the wounded Captain Marteen Zamora lay on the ground just yards away, his eyes narrow slits as he played dead, watching the three gringos mounting up. He swore to himself to remember every single detail about them, their height, the color of their hair, the horses they rode, the names they called each other.

The bullet lodged in his side burned like a white-hot poker, and his breath came in short gasps of pain, but Zamora would not die here. One by one his troops would eventually come back up the hill once they saw the Americans had left. When they did, he'd have them take him and the wagon to La Paz and help. He was determined to see the three gringos stood up against a wall and executed by a firing squad, if it was the last thing he ever did. He struggled up to a sitting position and began calling out for help.

*   *   *

When Trey, Joshua, and Luke reached the outskirts of La Paz just before dark, Trey told Joshua to take him to Chita's apartment, not back to the beach. Luke, still vengeful over Jack's cold-blooded murder, didn't know which way to run. He turned to Trey with a disgusted look on his face. "Well, now that this whole damn thing has blown up in our faces, what now?"

"Get out of La Paz, and quick." Trey leaned forward, the pain in his legs growing even worse. "They'll be looking for us all over. If you stay on the street you're going to get caught. You've got a double share of the money. Ride north."

Luke yanked his horse around, whipping it down the road as Trey turned back to Joshua. "Get me to Chita's fast, before I fall out of this saddle."

Chapter Twelve

Beach Ambush

By riding down side streets and back alleys, Trey and Joshua reached Chita's apartment just after sundown. "Can you make it up those stairs?" Joshua asked, getting down and coming to his side. Trey shook his head no. Joshua carefully pulled him down, wrapped his arm over his shoulder, and reached around with his other hand while grabbing him by his pants belt, as they started up the steep stairs. Trey groaned with each miserable step until they reached the top, and Joshua knocked rapidly on the door. When Chita opened it, her hands went to her mouth at the sight of Trey slumped against his pal.

"What happen!" she gasped, helping them both inside and quickly closing the door.

"Don't worry about that now. Trey needs a doctor and quick. He's got buckshot in both legs. It's gotta come out. I'm going back to the beach, and I'll take his horse with me. I'll take the saddlebags too except for what you need to pay a doctor." Joshua ran back downstairs to bring up one of the saddlebags. He unbuckled it, pouring money out on the table as Chita's eyes widened in disbelief.

"Where deed you get all dees *dinero*?"

"The same place Trey got shot up. Now don't ask me any more questions. Just go get help. I'll try to come back tomorrow if it looks all clear."

Joshua went out the door as Chita ran to the bed where Trey was laying. "I haf to get de *medico*. I be back as quick as I can." She kissed him lightly on the forehead, tears of fear in her eyes, before heading for the door.

Joshua rode out of town, then along the beach where surf hissed up on white sand while stars blinked in the nighttime sky over the blue Cortez. *How had things gone wrong,* he wondered to himself. Jack was dead, Trey was shot up so badly he was unable to ride or walk. The only thing left to do now was lay low for a while and hope the heat would pass. *Just give it time,* he thought. Maybe it would all straighten itself out, and then he and Trey could leave La Paz for good.

For the next two weeks Joshua spent his days staring at the village, riding into town only after dark to see how Trey was doing. A doctor had removed the buckshot from both his legs and bandaged him up from knee to hip. All he could do was lay in bed and stare at the ceiling as the pain throbbed deeper, while Chita tended him. She had stopped working at Casa Ramos until he could walk again.

The night Joshua arrived he met a girlfriend of hers named Juanita Moreno. Juanita, the same age as Chita, had long black hair and big inquisitive eyes, but was not as outgoing, especially around gringos. She could speak some English, but preferred to let someone else do most of the talking while glancing at Joshua's sky blue eyes and light, curly hair. She was taken with him from the very first night but tried not to let it show, until finally admitting it to Chita.

One evening when Chita decided to go out to buy something to eat instead of fixing it at her apartment, Joshua and Juanita were left alone in the kitchen while Trey slept in the other room.

"You leeve on the beach?" she finally asked. Joshua said he did, several miles out of town. "You like it there?" He said it was quiet, out of the way, and the rent was inexpensive.

"Would you like to ride out with me and take a look at it?" he asked, a boyish smile spreading across his face. She smiled back, without answering, but he already thought he had one.

Two evenings later after he left Trey and Chita, Juanita rode behind him, her hands around his waist, as they rode along the beach and a cool night wind lifted the surf in misty sheets of gold under a full moon. When they reached the line of darkened shacks, he lifted her down off the horse and held her there for a moment as their lips met for the first time. Then he swept her up in his arms, mounting the creaking stairs into the shack. It would not be their only night there. She was fascinated by the dashing young gringo with his air of confidence about everything he did and the fancy, pearl-handled pistols he always kept under his pillow while they slept.

Luke Estees didn't sleep as well in the center of La Paz at the federal police station. He lay on the floor of a dark, dank cell where he'd been imprisoned for two torturous weeks after being captured at a roadside checkpoint. He'd been beaten and starved to give up the names of his accomplices. Now he was near the breaking point. The ruthless *federales* were masters of torture and privation. They needed to solve the bold robbery and murder puzzle at the pay wagon, and Luke was their only link to doing it. If they had to kill him to get the answer, so be it.

A key rattled in the cell door and Luke rolled over as two armed guards came in. They dragged him to his feet and out the door and down the hall into the commander's office. Once inside he was handcuffed with his hands behind his back and legs manacled before being forced to sit in a chair facing a desk. On the other side Captain Marteen Zamora stared back at him without the slightest show of emotion, his arm in a sling and his side still bandaged from the gun battle on the road. Luke tried to focus on his face. His eyes were bleary from the beatings he'd taken. He blinked and shook his head slowly as the same question he'd been asked every day was asked again.

"Where are your amigos who robbed the pay wagon weeth you, gringo?" Luke's head dropped to his chest as his breath came in a slow hiss. "I—don't—know. I—told you—that before."

Zamora snapped out an order to the guards. *"Agua!"* Luke was suddenly lifted from the chair, dragged across the room, and forced to kneel in front of a tub of water. A powerful hand grabbed him by the hair, forcing his face down into the water as he kicked and struggled to breathe. He choked as water rushed into his mouth and down his throat. His breath ran out, and he couldn't hold it any longer. Suddenly his world spun into blackness.

When he regained consciousness he was laying on his back with guards standing over him, and the same question was repeated. Again he said he didn't know before being yanked back up, dragged over to the tub, and plunged in again.

This time the blackness came faster. He couldn't take anymore. He couldn't even struggle. Luke had nothing left. He was done.

When he came to, the same insistent question drummed in

his ears. "Where are your companeros? I don't ask again. Next time you die."

Luke slumped in the chair as a lantern was brought close to his bruised and battered face while dark shadows leaned closer, waiting for the answer. Luke's mouth moved but at first nothing came out but spittle and water. He coughed, trying again. "Maybe—one's—down on the beach." His head fell forward on his chest until a hand grabbed him by the hair, pulling him back up. "I—don't know—about the other—one. In town someplace."

Minutes later outside in the dark, a dozen federal police led by Zamora mounted up and thundered down the street, heading for the Cortez shoreline. Zamora felt a surge of adrenaline pumping through his body as he gouged spurs into his steed's side. At last he had something to go on and a chance to restore his reputation after the humiliation he'd suffered at the hands of the gringos. He meant to extract every last measure of it in revenge.

Joshua and Juanita had spent the evening in town with Trey and Chita, staying late. Trey was recovering, up and able to walk around, the pain diminishing and slowly fading away in his legs. They had briefly discussed leaving La Paz as soon as Trey could, but what they hadn't talked about was the women and whether they would they leave them or not.

Four people riding together was easily noticed, especially when two of them were women. Should they stay in Mexico or cross the border back into the States? They were wanted in both countries. Trey took Joshua by the arm, walking him out on the porch and closing the door behind him so they were alone. "Soon as I can ride, I think we ought to clear out. There's no telling if Luke made it or not. If he didn't, we could both be in for big trouble. As far as the girls go, I don't know what to do about them. Just watch yourself for the next few days until I think I can ride again. It won't take too long."

Joshua smiled back. "I can take care of myself if trouble comes along. You ought to know that by now."

"Yeah, I do. But not if the *federales* come at you a dozen at a time. Just be careful, like I said. Maybe I'll try and ride out to the village in a day or two to see how I feel."

After Joshua and Juanita left, Chita walked Trey over to the bed and sat on the edge. She had that look in her eye that Trey had seen before. It was the look of suspicion he was trying to keep something from her, like right now. She turned his face to hers using both hands and stared straight into his eyes. He started to cut her off by saying something, but she was quicker, putting her finger on his lips to stop him.

"Are you going to leave me, Trey?"

For a moment he couldn't answer. He tried to think of a quick response but she asked again before he could. He took in a deep breath, staring back at her. "Look, Chita—I might have to run for it if things fall apart. You always knew that could happen, didn't you? You know what I do for a living. I've never made any secret of it. I won't have any choice if things turn sour."

"Yes, you do—you can take me weeth you. I go anywhere you want."

Trey looked away, rubbing the back of his neck in exasperation. This was exactly what he didn't want to hear. He turned back, grabbing her by both shoulders. "You can't ride a thousand miles with me, maybe having to fight it out every mile of the way. We might even have to cross the border back into the States. Can't you understand that?"

But Chita wasn't done yet. "You cannot leave me." Tears began to well up in her eyes as Trey pulled her close, trying to end the argument. Then he made the mistake of asking her why. "Because—I am going to have your baby."

Juanita rode with her arms around Joshua's waist and her head against his shoulder as they moved along the beach toward the fishing village. Rhythmic waves washing up on the sand had a calming hiss that all was well. Neither spoke, each with their own thoughts, though romance wasn't on Joshua's mind. Trey's warning about leaving and his own bravado scoffing at it were all show. Trey was right. What if Luke didn't make it out of La Paz? He tried to shrug it off, reaching over his shoulder to cradle Juanita's head against him.

Up ahead, the outline of shacks were painted in a soft glow from the silver moon. It was a welcome sight. Joshua was tired and so was his woman. A good night's sleep would make tomorrow look better again. He reined to a halt and lifted her down, starting up the plank stairs with her hand in his. Once inside, he unbuckled his pistols, slid out of his boots, pants, and shirt, laying on the mat as Juanita did the same. As she pulled a single light sheet over them, Joshua rolled over, sliding his pearl-handled pistols under his pillow.

Juanita rose up on one elbow and kissed him on the lips. He started to say no, but she kissed him again. Her warm body felt good against him. Her wet mouth tasted of woman and lingering tequila. Maybe sleep could wait just a little longer tonight. After all, tomorrow they could swim and stretch out on the beach in the sun if they wanted to rest.

The moon traced its ageless arc across a star-scattered sky on its way to disappear into the blue Cortez. Joshua did not hear the squeak of boots ascending the platform steps outside as the shadows of men moved toward the door. Captain Zamora held up his hand for silence while lifting his pistol, slowly pulling back the curtain entrance and peering in. Moonglow lit the man and woman sleeping inside. Her body matched the curve of his. Zamora started to step inside, the rattan floor squeaking under his heavy boots. Joshua's eyes instantly opened and he rolled over, his hand darting under the pillow for the pearl-handled pistols. The deafening roar of six handguns spitting spears of flame and hot lead stopped him, shattering the silence of the shack as bullets cut into Joshua and Juanita until neither one moved and their blood dripped on the rattan floor. Joshua Logan, the Mormon desperado, would never see Utah again.

The next morning Chita worked her way through the side-street carts and vendors shopping for food. At one cart, three women were talking excitedly about the shootings at the fishing village the previous evening. Chita stopped, staring at the three, coming closer to ask what happened. When she was told a gringo bandito and his Mexican woman were killed by the federal police, her hand went to her mouth in horror. She immediately turned, running for her apartment. Reaching it, she vaulted up the stairs and burst through the door. "Trey—Trey, where are you?!"

Trey was in the bedroom laying down but quickly came to his feet at her urgent call. They met in the front room, where she threw her arms around him, still out of breath as he questioned her. "What's the matter? Why are you so upset?"

She quickly told him of the news she'd heard down on the street. Trey pushed her back with both hands and his eyes narrowed. "Are you sure of this?" She nodded, tears beginning to run down her cheeks not only for Joshua and Juanita, but now Trey and herself too.

"Weel they keel us too?" she asked, her breath catching in her throat.

"Not if I can help it. Pack your things right now. We've got to get out of here before the police find us too. They must have found out where Joshua was from Luke Estees. I knew I couldn't trust that bastard. Hurry, get your stuff together!"

Half an hour later Trey and Chita approached the livery stable where he kept his horse. He bought a second horse and saddle for her, telling the owner to get ready fast, without ever asking her if she could even ride. They tied their belongings behind the saddle, filling both saddlebags too. When he saw her reach up and grab the saddle horn, putting her foot in the stirrup and deftly swinging up, he had his answer. She had seen the question in his eyes too.

"My *padre* had *los caballos* when I was a leetle girl. I know how to ride."

A grim smile briefly crossed Trey's face. He'd made his decision to bring her with him, even though he knew if things got tight and he had to fight his way out, she could be a burden. The only other thing he was certain of was that she was carrying his child, and that was something he could not leave behind in La Paz. Just short of twenty years old, he was going to be a father. The other thought that crossed his mind was, would he live long enough to ever see this baby?

"You ready?" He stared hard at Chita for just a moment. She nodded back, fear still plain in her eyes. "Then let's ride!"

Chapter Thirteen

Road North

The pair of fleeing riders streaked through the outskirts of La Paz, then out past the last adobe-walled houses into dry, barren hills on the road leading north. As he rode Trey kept thinking about Luke. The *federales* could have captured him on this very same road. The more he thought about it, the more he was sure he was right. After an hour of hard riding he signaled for Chita to pull to a halt. "Let's leave the road at least for a couple of days until I'm sure we're in the clear. We'll ride along the beach down there." He pointed to the white line of breakers washing the shore.

They reined their animals down through cactus-covered slopes, heading for the cool blue of the Cortez. Reaching it, they rode all that day along the beach, fronted by steep, rocky cliffs. When evening came they stopped, making camp under a rocky outcrop, not daring to burn a fire.

That same afternoon back in La Paz, Captain Zamora walked slowly through Chita Ovalis' apartment, directing his men to ransack the place while he searched for anything that might tell him where she and her gringo boyfriend had fled to. Juanita Moreno's body had been identified by her grief-stricken mother who also told the captain that her daughter spent many nights at the house of her best friend, Chita. The police emptied every drawer and cabinet, but it was Zamora who found the bloodstains on the bed when he threw back the covers. That's when he remembered the Americano wounded in the payroll robbery. Now he was certain the fourth and last bandit must have been here. The other three were already dead. He'd had Luke Estees stood up against the prison wall and executed by his firing squad.

The captain found a garbage bag under the sink and poured out everything in it on the table. He sat separating the refuge piece by piece. He lifted out one small scrap of paper, brushing food particles off it to read the blurred writing. It was part of a shipping bill for ore delivered at Porto Oro, off Loyal Quinn's ship, the *Dorado*.

Zamora got to his feet, walked to the window, and stared out as his mind raced. Was the last of the bandits heading north for Porto Oro to try to escape? Obviously he had come through there at some point. He decided to play a hunch, turning to his men, shouting new orders to stop everything and get to their horses. The *federales* would ride north too, at a break-neck pace, to see if they could run down the last gringo killer.

When dawn came, Trey and Chita saddled up again, riding their horses along the rocky coastline. They spent that day making the best time they could, but often had to double back and climb over rocky cliffs that ran straight down into the sea. By day's end the strain of the murderous pace began to show in Chita, even though she did not complain. That's when Trey decided the next morning they'd abandon the coast and head for the road paralleling it several miles above where the going would be easier, even though it was more risky if they were being followed. The thought that somehow the federal police might have found out where he and Chita were heading had worried him since they had left La Paz. Throughout the day he'd continually glanced back behind them to see if anyone was following. He saw no one, nor any plume of dust that many riders were coming hard. Still, he couldn't get the nagging thought out of his mind.

Far back Zamora was coming hard, whipping his tired horse and men forward as his eyes raced ahead searching for some sign of the two riders. Twice he'd stopped travelers but they were not the pair he wanted. When evening came, Zamora did not stop. Instead, he told his men to stay in the saddle and push their mounts to the breaking point.

After sundown, Trey pulled a short distance off the road and helped Chita down. She leaned on him for support as he wrapped both arms around her, kissing her lightly on the cheek. He knew she was dead tired from the hard riding, but they had to try and keep up the pace.

"Here, sit down and I'll get you a blanket off my horse." He retrieved it, spreading it on the ground as she curled up in it and he folded the other half over her. "Try to get some rest, hon. I'm going to stay up for a while." He sat watching her until her eyes closed, and she fell quickly into a deep sleep. How far were they from Porto Oro? he wondered. He tried to remember the ride down, but the memory of the Mormon schoolboy he'd taken on as a partner, now lying dead back in La Paz, blocked everything else out. He'd grown close to Joshua, closer than he thought he ever could.

Now he was dead. Were he and Chita going to end up the

same way? She was carrying his child, something he'd never given a moment's thought to until she'd announced it days earlier. It changed everything. So much was changing so fast, it was almost impossible to keep up with it and stay one step ahead of disaster. But there was one thing Trey Wingo was certain of. He and his woman had to get to Porto Oro and across the Sea of Cortez to mainland Mexico at all cost.

Trey stayed up most of that night. He was able to doze off a little during the two hours before dawn, and when he opened his eyes the sky was already turning bright blue. He got to his feet, staring back down the still-empty road.

"Chita, it's time to go. Come on, honey, get up. We've got to leave." He helped her to her feet and up on her horse. Moments later they were riding north again at a steady gallop.

The sun was scorching hot at midday when up ahead Trey saw what looked like two wagons. As they drew closer he saw it was a pair loaded with cattle hides. He glanced over at Chita, clinging doggedly to the saddle horn, tired but refusing to complain as they caught up with the freighters.

"Hola." Trey forced a smile, stretching his Mexican vocabulary to the limit as the wagon drivers pulled their teams to a halt. "Do you speak any English?" Both drivers shook their heads. He turned to Chita. "Ask them how far it is to Porto Oro."

As she was doing so, Trey looked down the road. This time, instead of an empty trail shimmering in heat waves, he saw the blurred image of many riders coming fast, marked by a rising cloud of dust. As Chita turned to tell him Porto Oro was another two days' ride away, he pointed at the riders, eyes narrowed in concern. "That looks like trouble. There's too many of them to be anything but the *federales,* and we can't outrun them now. Ask these drivers if you can ride with them. Tell them we just got married and your father is trying to stop us from leaving or anything else you can think of. Quick, hon, while we've still got a few minutes left."

Chita had a brief conversation with the lead driver. He nodded, helping her climb onto the wagon seat next to him. Trey shouted a quick good-bye, kicking his horse off the road toward the beach a mile away, towing Chita's mount behind him.

Captain Zamora whipped his sweat-covered horse ahead faster, eyes riveted on the wagons moving ahead. They were the first travelers he'd seen in over a day. He glanced over his shoulder at his men, who were strung out in a long, scattered line behind him. Both men and horses were stretched to the breaking point at this murderous pace. If he didn't find the gringo and his woman soon, he might have to admit to himself that the long ride had been for nothing.

"Parada!" Zamora shouted, coming up alongside the lead wagon as the driver pulled back on the reins, bringing the freighter to a clattering halt. "Do you travel alone?" he asked.

"Yes, I do." The old man nodded, pushing the straw hat back on his head, as Zamora ordered his men to dismount and go through the wagons.

"Where are you bound?" Zamora questioned.

"Porto Oro. We sell these hides there for shipment to Guaymas. Will you accompany us, Captain?"

The captain waited until his men were finished, having not found anything, then turned back to the old man. "I have no time for that. I'm looking for a gringo and his Mexican woman. Have you seen them on this road in your travels?"

"No." The driver shook his head. "You are the only ones I have seen since leaving La Paz." He wondered to himself why the federal police would be sent all this way just to return a runaway daughter eloping with an American, but held his tongue.

Zamora took off his hat, wiped the sweat from his face in frustration, then twisted in the saddle to talk to his men. "Mount up. We ride for Porto Oro. Quickly!"

As the line of tan-clad federales sped away in a cloud of dust, the wagon driver sat watching them go until they were nearly out of sight. A small voice came from behind him. "Can I come out now?" He turned in the seat, pulling back the hide cover of a small compartment that held food and water plus some tools. He helped Chita slowly untangle herself, squeezing out until she sat on the seat next to him, straightening her hair and brushing herself to face her benefactor and his questioning face.

"You and your gringo friend must have done something very bad to have the federal police come all this way looking for you."

She stared back for a moment, trying to think of an excuse, then put a hand on his shoulder. "We love each other very much. I'm going to have his baby. That is all you need to know. Were you not young once too?"

A slow smile spread across the old man's face and he shrugged, snapping the reins down as the mules pulled in their traces and the wagon lurched forward.

All that day Trey shadowed the wagons, staying close to the rocky coastline. The going here was slower, cliffs sloping straight down into the ocean, forcing him to double back time and again to catch up. That evening as the Yucatán sun made its final plunge into the Cortez, Trey cautiously reined his horse back up toward the road. As he came into sight of the wagon, Chita stood up waving, a smile of relief brightening her tired face until he was alongside, and they leaned to kiss each other. The driver glanced at them, remembering her words earlier about his own youth and past loves.

"You tell your gringo we stop for the night just ahead," he

said, nodding down the road. "You should also tell him to-morrow afternoon we reach Porto Oro."

The wagons were pulled next to each other, and while the mules were being unbuckled from their traces, the other driver got a small fire going. By the time the sky filled with sparkling stars, a pot of beans was bubbling away over the fire and tortillas were heating on a thin steel plate.

Trey sat leaning back against a wagon wheel, taking in slow breaths with his arm around Chita as she rested her head on his shoulder, relaxing for the first time that day.

"You tired?" he asked, squeezing her slender shoulder.

"Maybe a leetle beet. But I'll be all right as long as you are safe. José says tomorrow we weel reach Porto Oro. Then what do we do?"

"What we'll do is pray we can stay away from the *federales*. There isn't much there and it's not easy to stay out of sight. I have a friend who owns a ship, if he's there. It's the same one I came over on. If Quinn's in port, we'll hide out on it until we can get to the mainland. After that I think we'll be okay."

Chita looked up at Trey and slowly ran her hand through his hair. She'd abandoned everything and everyone to come with him: her mother, father, and two younger sisters. Of all the men who had flirted and tried to take her out, she'd fallen for this young Americano instead. Even with the federal police breathing down the back of their necks and her being pregnant, she would stay by his side. She couldn't help but wonder what tomorrow would bring, when they reached the port. Whatever it might be, she held her tongue. For tonight, with a warm, crackling fire and her man close against her, she would not break this brief spell of happiness.

Chapter Fourteen

Good-bye, Yucatán

At the first hint of dawn Trey quietly slid out from under the blanket, carefully pulling it back over Chita, who was still sleeping. He stood and turned toward the ocean as cotton-ball clouds with dark bottoms drifted inland on a cooling wind. The drivers, under the blankets, slept too. He walked away from the wagons, strapping on his gun belt and pulling his pistol, checking to be certain all six cylinders were full. Today he knew he'd have to use them. Trey went to the saddle scabbard to check the rifle too.

Once they reached town there wouldn't be time for any of this. He walked back to the smoldering pile of ashes from last night's fire, kneeling to feed it a few fresh sticks. A small puff of flame leaped to life as he warmed his hands, but a shiver of cold coursed through his body. He hoped it was only from the morning chill and not a case of nerves.

An hour later the wagons were rumbling down the road, but this time Chita was riding next to him. She had to be. If they were forced to move fast, they had to be together. Trey was

120

gambling everything on the *Dorado* being in port. If it wasn't, they would have to either hide out, fight, or run for it.

As they rode farther north, the tension mounted with each mile, until that afternoon when the curve of the bay came into view up ahead. Trey reined to a halt, standing in the stirrups and squinting to study the distant dock. Shielding his eyes against the sun, he saw a ship was in port, but he still wasn't sure if it was the *Dorado*. "We've got to get closer." His voice was low with concern. "Tell José thanks for the ride. We'll go ahead from here on our own."

Chita bid the old man adios, and they urged their horses forward at a gallop. Half an hour later Trey was certain it was the *Dorado*. All he had to do now was find Quinn and ask him when he was leaving for the mainland. At the outskirts of town they abandoned the road, turning to ride along the shore-line shacks to keep out of sight. The *federales* had to be in town someplace, but as they moved closer they still didn't see them. There was a good reason why.

Captain Zamora and his men had already scoured Porto Oro from one end to the other looking for the gringo and his woman. Puzzled at not finding them, Zamora worried if they'd possibly bypassed the town and were still riding north. As he struggled with himself on what to do next, he told his men to continue searching while he stopped at a local cantina to cool off. The relentless summer sun and his lack of success had him snapping at everyone when he pushed through the door of the Swordfish Cantina.

The first man he saw sitting at the bar was an Americano, but obviously not the one he wanted. He was older, heavier, a big man with an unruly salt-and-pepper beard. He wore a dirty shirt and tattered captain's hat. Loyal Quinn slowly turned from his drink, studying the officer as Zamora called out for a bottle of mescal. Turning back to the barman, Quinn whispered, "What's the federal police doing here in Porto Oro?" The barman shrugged, eyes wide and hands palm up.

If there was one thing Quinn didn't like it was the law. He never adhered to rules and regulations or those that enforced them. That was one of the main reasons he'd moved to Mexico. He was free to do what he pleased without interference. He turned his glass up, finished his drink, and pushed money across the counter. Heading for the door, he passed the captain and noticed his narrow face was beaded with sweat. His grim mouth was outlined by a pencil-thin mustache, and it was clear the officer was twisting over something. As he stepped out into the street, Quinn saw more *federales* going door-to-door. He wondered what all the excitement was about. He was going to find out a lot faster than he ever dreamed possible.

Trey and Chita had ridden as close to the dock as they dared when they saw the first policeman moving down a narrow street nearby. They immediately dismounted, and Trey pushed her into a backyard looking for some way out. On a low adobe wall surrounding the yard, freshly washed clothes were drying. Trey grabbed a brightly colored *serape*, swinging it over his shoulders. By the back door a big straw sombrero was hung on a hook. He put it on, pulling it low across his face. "Come on." He grabbed Chita by the arm, rushing her through the small house past a startled old man and woman sitting in the front room and out the door into the dirt street.

Three uniformed officers were questioning a man across the street as Trey and Chita quickly turned their backs to them and hurried away. One of the *federales* turned as they passed, studying the pair. For a moment, he didn't say anything, then he elbowed his partner. Both took a few steps forward, watching the man and woman. *"Parada!"* one shouted and raised his hand, but Trey and his woman kept walking without turning around.

"Don't stop," Trey whispered, his hand slipping under the *serape* and lifting his pistol from its holster, as the three *federales* began running toward them, still shouting. As their footsteps drew closer until they were nearly on top of them, Trey suddenly pushed Chita aside, turning in one swift motion at a crouch, his pistol clearing the *serape*. The wheel gun spit murderous fire once, twice, three times in quick succession, catching the officers off guard. Too late to fire back, all three crumpled to the ground. Trey grabbed Chita by the hand, and they fled down a narrow side street at a run, heading for the dock.

Two blocks uphill in the Swordfish Cantina, Zamora heard the muffled shots and quickly stood. He pulled his pistol, shouting for the two officers with him to follow as he ran out the front door. Across the street, five more of his men were going from house to house until he shouted at them to follow him. They all ran downhill toward the shots.

Loyal Quinn had just reached the wharf and was walking out to his ship when he heard the shots echoing from the streets above. He stopped and turned to scan the row of houses, wondering if the officers he'd just seen in the cantina had anything to do with the sudden gunfire. One thing he knew for certain was that it had to spell trouble, and he was leaving Porto Oro anyway after offloading another supply of ore. He quickened his pace down the wharf toward his ship. The sooner he cleared the dock the better. After stepping onboard he yelled for his deckhands to start the engine and prepare to leave. While they headed below he climbed the steel ladder up to the wheelhouse, then stood on the platform outside looking back toward town, listening for more shots.

On one of those streets Trey and Chita were running for their lives, but she could barely keep up as they dodged between buildings and Trey pulled her along. When they ran around another corner he stopped, propping her up in his arms. Her tortured eyes stared up at him, then she spoke. "Trey—I cannot run any longer." Tears began sliding down her face. "You must go on without me—or dey weel catch you."

Trey took a quick peek around the corner. More *federales* were running toward them. He leveled his pistol against the building, steadied it, and opened up, again scattering the officers for a moment before quickly reloading. His mind raced for an answer.

"I'm not going to leave you." He was almost shouting. "Listen to me. We've got to make it to the ship or we're done for. You run for it while I hold them off here. Tell Quinn who you are and that I'm coming as fast as I can, you understand? Tell him to wait for me. Now get going and hurry. It's the only chance we've got!" Chita started to resist but he pushed her away, insisting again that she reach the *Dorado*. Suddenly the ship's whistle sounded with three long toots. "Go!" Trey's voice was a harsh whisper. She turned and ran.

Trey knelt and leaned against the wall as he peeked around the corner, pushing the six-gun out in front of him and opening up with a barrage of shots that sent the approaching *federales* scurrying for cover. A block away, Captain Zamora—still running—heard the shooting and changed direction, heading for it as he yelled for his men to follow him.

As the standoff continued, Chita finally reached the dock, barely able to stay on her feet from exhaustion. She waved her hand wildly while running toward the ship. Quinn leaned forward, squinting at the tiny figure of a woman coming closer. He stepped out of the wheelhouse and came down the ladder onto the dock as she reached him, collapsing in his arms. "Who are you?" He lifted her chin, still supporting her with one arm.

"Trey says . . . for you to . . . wait for heem. You cannot go until he make eet here."

He lifted her and stared down at her. "Trey? You mean Trey Wingo?" His eyes widened in disbelief as Chita nodded, too out of breath to speak. He brought her onboard and turned, yelling for one of his men to take her down below while he cast off the mooring lines.

Back up on the street, Trey held off the police using the building corner as a shield, firing whenever one of the *federales* showed himself. He wondered if Chita had made it to the ship yet. He couldn't stay here much longer. He'd have to make a run for it himself and quick, before they flanked him.

Captain Zamora came down an alley behind him, and when the captain peeked around the corner, Trey was only thirty yards away. He had his back to him, completely unaware he was wide open for a shot. Captain Zamora leaned around the corner, gripping his pistol with both hands and lining up the sights on the unsuspecting Americano. He couldn't miss at this distance. He slowly squeezed the trigger until the pistol bucked in his hands and ran forward to put in finishing shots.

Trey spun on his knees, the bullet cutting through the *serape* but not breaking skin. The captain was coming fast. They fired nonstop at the same time, the shots sounding like one endless roar. The officer stopped twenty feet away and swayed on his feet, still trying to squeeze the trigger as he slowly sagged to the ground and fell on his face with two bullet holes in his chest.

Trey leaped to his feet, darting down an alley and reloading the pistol as he ran. Down on the *Dorado,* Loyal Quinn stabbed at the ship's whistle once, twice, three times. Where was the kid? he wondered. Quinn couldn't stay docked much longer. Suddenly he saw a lone figure break out of the last buildings onto the wharf, running for all he was worth with his *serape* flapping out behind him. The figure was halfway down the dock when Quinn saw a dozen *federales* exit from the same buildings, running after the *serape* man and firing as they went. It had to be Trey.

Quinn shifted the ship into reverse, and it slowly began moving along the wharf toward its end as Trey streaked closer. He leaned out the wheelhouse door yelling, "Run, boy, run. I can't hold her here much longer!"

Bullets splintered the planks around Trey's feet as he neared the end of the dock, barely able to breathe. His lungs were on fire, and his legs felt like they were going to give out from under him. The *Dorado* cleared the last pilings the same instant Trey did. He leaped in the air, arms flailing for distance, suspended as if in slow motion, until crashing down on the deck and rolling to a stop.

Quinn gunned the ship's engine and the *Dorado* surged farther from the wooden platform as the policemen came to a halt, still firing at the departing vessel. Bullets splintered its wooden hull and deck, but the old hull soaked them up without damage. When the ship was well out from the shore, Quinn spun the wheel, bringing her around bow first and gunning the engine forward. Then he stepped out the wheelhouse door, looking down on his passenger and shaking his head as Trey slowly got to his feet, taking off the big sombrero while wiping the sweat from his face, the gun still gripped in his other hand.

"Well, boy, you sure know how to get yourself a lot of attention, don't you? And where's your friend Joshua?" Quinn's beard parted in a slow smile, as the young gun stared back at him.

"He didn't make it. That bunch you saw chasing me caught up to him in La Paz. I wasn't going to let them do the same to me and Chita. She is onboard, isn't she?"

Quinn nodded. "Yes, I have your 'cargo' down below, safe and sound. Did you bring anything else of value with you? Those *federales* weren't chasing you for nothing, were they?"

Trey slid out of the *serape* and let it fall to the deck, then pointed at the bulging money belt around his waist. "I thought so." Quinn nodded. "In that case you can pay me for passage for two to the mainland. I won't charge extra for saving your skin, though. We'll just chalk that up to old friendship!"

Chapter Fifteen

Home Again

As the *Dorado* was cutting its way through Cortez waters, over a thousand miles north Johnny was staring out the window of a cold cell in Montana's Territorial Prison. As he'd promised Trey, Johnny had whisked Laura Logan away in the black of night, leaving Utah behind and riding back for Montana and his home. When he arrived two months later, his grief-stricken mother and father rejoiced at seeing him still alive after not hearing a word from him all the time he was gone. The moment Johnny and Laura had crossed over into Wyoming, they had married at a justice of the peace in Rock Springs. Now the Blades not only had a returning son, but a new daughter-in-law to boot, something unexpected but thrilling nonetheless.

After greeting the pair with hugs and tears, Howard and Ida turned to the question of the killings in Eagleville. Johnny admitted the letter he'd left when he and Trey ran away was the truth. He'd pulled a trigger just like his friend had. That's when Howard insisted Johnny turn himself in, tell the entire story of events leading up to the shootings, and face the punishment.

Trey's father had been murdered and his brother was crippled for life. Sheriff Gibber had done nothing about it, and that drove the young men to take the law into their own hands.

"We don't have to go to Eagleville or Loyalton with this, son. We can go down to Helena where they've got some decent law. As far as Gibber goes, he's out of the picture anyway. He died last year not long after you and Trey left."

"Gibber is dead?" Johnny's eyes widened in disbelief.

"Yes, and I say good riddance, considering the way that fool rode out to the Wingo ranch with his deputy and confronted Samantha, Frank, and Trey."

"How did he die?" Johnny leaned forward and ran his hands through his hair, still scarcely believing what he was hearing.

"He died in the Buckhorn Bar. Pretty fitting, from what I've been told. He had a drink, turned around to leave, and collapsed on the floor. They took him over to the jail and got Doc Feeney, but he couldn't help him. He was already too far gone."

"If Trey knew that, there's a good chance he might come back here too," Johnny said.

"I don't know if it would do him any good. From what I've heard the law wants him for more than just the shootings down in Eagleville. But you're a different story. If you turn yourself in in Helena, I'll even hire a lawyer to defend you. Those three men you and Trey shot down in Eagleville were wanted for armed robbery and two murders. You two did the territory a favor, just in the wrong way. I know it's not easy to think about turning yourself in now, with Laura and all, but it's the only way to clear your name for the rest of your life. You cannot live looking over your shoulder every day like Trey will."

Johnny turned to his mother and put a hand on her shoulder. "Mom, before I do anything else, I've got to ride over to the

Wingo ranch and talk to Samantha and Frank. They don't know anything about Trey and I do, at least up to a point. I've got to tell them what I know."

Rachel stepped forward and wrapped her arms around Johnny, tears suddenly flooding her eyes. "Of course you should, hon. And I know they both will appreciate anything you can tell them about Trey, the poor boy. Just wait until tomorrow. You and Laura stay home for tonight. There's still so much we have to ask you."

Johnny gave her a big hug, then took Laura by the hand to walk outside and watch the sun go down. Up on the ridges above the ranch, leaves of quaking aspen were blinking gold and crimson in the evening breeze. Fall was already in the air. He turned, facing Laura with a serious stare. "If I do go to prison, I'll miss you every second I'm gone, but you'll stay here with my ma and pa until I get out. That way I won't have to worry about you."

Laura stepped close, holding him tight and whispering in his ear. "I'll be all right, Johnny, but I do wonder about my brother, Joshua. I know my mother and father will be worried about him too, even though my father was so strict with him. And there is something else I should tell you."

"What's that, hon?"

"I think . . . I'm not sure yet . . . but I think I'm going to have a baby," she said with an uneasy smile.

Johnny held her back at arm's length, a look of sheer amazement spreading over his face. His mouth opened but he couldn't find the right words. He took in a deep breath, trying again. "You're . . . not sure? I mean . . . when will you be?"

"In another month, maybe." She cupped his face in her hands, smiling. "I just thought I should bring it up now before you decide what you're going to do about turning yourself in, that's all."

Johnny stepped back and took in a deep breath, trying to make some sense of it all. How could he go to prison if Laura actually was pregnant? He'd be in jail while his child was being born, and he wouldn't even be there to help her raise it. He pulled Laura close to him again and they hugged each other, but Johnny said no more. Now he had two things to worry about.

The next morning Johnny saddled up to ride for the Wingo ranch as he'd promised. When he arrived, he saw Frank outside chopping kindling. Frost was in the air, and it was time to get the winter supply of wood stacked on the front porch before the first snowfall. Frank heard hoofbeats coming closer and turned, using the axe as a cane, and walked across the yard to the hitching rail. The bullet wound had left him with a permanent limp. As the rider drew closer, he thought he looked like Johnny Blades, but that couldn't be. A minute later he was stunned to see that he was right, it was Johnny. Frank turned, calling for Samantha to come quick.

When Johnny pulled to a stop and dismounted, they came together in a big bear hug, all trying to talk at the same time. "Johnny, for God's sake, it's good to see you, boy!" Frank slapped him on the back as Samantha kissed him on the cheek, her eyes aching with the questions only Johnny could answer.

"Is my boy with you, Johnny? Is he all right?"

Johnny shook his head, taking her hands in his. "I'm sorry, ma'am, but I rode over here to tell you I haven't seen Trey in a long time. When he left Utah, he was okay though."

"Utah!" Samantha's eyes widened. "Please come inside and tell me all about this. There's no need for us to stand out here in the cold."

An hour later Johnny had told Samantha and Frank the entire story since he and Trey had fled. They both sat staring at him, stunned to silence about all that had happened to the pair, until Samantha spoke up. "If Trey told you he was riding south, how far do you think he meant to go?"

Johnny shrugged and shook his head. "I really don't know." He wished he could be more helpful, but he couldn't. Secretly he wondered if Trey was even still alive, but he wouldn't say so out loud. When he got up to leave, Samantha hugged him at the front door and Frank shook his hand, thanking him for riding over and telling them what he could.

Two weeks later, Johnny, Laura, and his parents made the three-day ride to Helena. Howard had convinced Johnny to turn himself in and get it over with, rather than live his life always looking over his shoulder. Judge Beamer heard the case with interest without a jury. Sheriff Gibber was dead, but Sheriff Todd from Eagleville was summoned and made the long trip there to testify. The unsolved killings of the three men in the nighttime street fight had haunted him since the event took place. Now one of the men involved was finally admitting his involvement. He wanted to see at least part of the case settled for his own peace of mind.

The trial was concluded in just one day. At its end, Johnny was convicted of murder with extenuating circumstances. Judge Beamer did not want to see him put away for ten years; he was too young. He seemed to be a decent-enough young man who simply got carried away by events he had little control over. The judge called Johnny to the bench, as Rachel and Laura wept silently on either side of Howard while he put both arms around their shoulders.

Beamer leveled a gaze at Johnny over glasses perched on the end of his nose. "Son, I understand the situation you found yourself in and your desire to help your friend, this man named Trey Wingo, who should really be facing this court today. But even though the men you are charged with helping kill were, in fact, fugitives from the law themselves, you still took their lives wantonly. This point cannot be overlooked. We must all live by the letter of the law. I'm going to sentence you to three years in the territorial prison with time off for good behavior. You walk the straight and narrow, you could gain your freedom before that time is served. If you do not, you'll serve every single day of it. This court has noted that you elected to turn yourself in and face punishment. That has given you some important support in my sentence. I'm also going to write the warden a letter on your behalf. I wish you well in the time ahead. Do what you have to now, then go back home and live the decent life you were meant to. This court is now adjourned."

Johnny stood on the iron-railed bed in his cell, both hands gripping the bars for support while staring out the window. It was snowing again, and the dark, gray clouds were nearly blotted out by a blizzard of big, white snowflakes cascading down. Judge Beamer's words still rung in his ears, about doing his sentence without incident and getting out of prison early. It had been only three months since he'd been sent here, yet it seemed like three long years. He wondered if he could actually survive three years without going mad, or worse.

He thought constantly about home, Laura, their unborn baby, his mom, dad, and sometimes even Trey. Where was he now? What had happened to him after all this time? The prison yard was covered with a fresh blanket of new white, and he knew back home the house, barn, and corral would be too. The gnawing thought of not being there almost drove him wild. He hung his head and closed his eyes, gripping the bars so tight his knuckles turned bone white as a shudder of emotion swept over him.

Far to the south across the border in Mexico, the sun was shining brightly in the tiny mountain town of Pequeño Colina. Trey and Chita had ridden there after reaching the mainland at Los Mochis. Trey's original plan to ride north across the border out of Mexico was abandoned when Chita learned that the *federales* were looking all over Mexico for them.

Chita was young, but the long ride trying to outrun the *federales* was beginning to take its toll on her physically and mentally. She needed to rest before they tried to ride north again, and the small scattering of adobe homes around the dirt main street of the sleepy little village was exactly the kind of out-of-the-way place to do so. The *federales* would be looking for the pair in big cities like Hermosillo and Guaymas, not here. They rented a small cottage overlooking the village perched on the rim of a hill, to wait things out. For the first two weeks Trey sat for hours on the front porch looking down the road leading up to the cottage, his rifle on the small table in front of him in case they had sudden unwelcome visitors wearing tan uniforms. By the third week he'd relaxed and went inside, sitting by the window after taking off his six-gun and hanging it on a peg by the front door.

The quiet scene below never seemed to change. The Mexican sun baked the tile rooftops of the homes, while a few people walked the street to the general store. The village was quiet except for an occasional crowing of a rooster and the sound of children laughing as they played. Life moved at the same slow pace it had in Pequeño Colina for over a century.

On Sunday church bells rang, calling parishioners to gather and pray to God for good crops, winter rains to water them, and salvation for all mortal souls teetering on the brink of hell.

Those same bells began to move something in Chita, for one Sunday about a month later, she asked Trey if they could attend services.

"Are you crazy?" he shot back. "We're trying to stay out of sight, not show up in church. I'm the gringo, remember? I stick out like a sore thumb anywhere we go. And since when did you start going to church anyway?"

Chita saw the alarm on his face as she came forward to wrap her arms around him. She pulled him close as she stared up at him with her big brown eyes. "My *madre* always took me to de church when I was a leetle girl. You try to understand dis, Trey. I want my baby baptized in de church when eet is born whereever we are. Maybe I'm no child of God, but I want our baby to be one."

Trey stared back, his face a puzzled mask, trying to understand why something like this could be so important when they were running for their lives. He locked her face in both his hands and looked down at her. "You know what I did the last time I was in a church?" Chita tried shaking her head but he held it tight. "I robbed it of every cent I could. That's what I think churches are good for."

"Den you are wrong. Whatever we now are, I want our niño to be de child of God. Eet will not haf to run and hide as we do. Can I go now without you?" Her eyes were steady, unblinking.

"Go ahead, but remember to keep quiet about us. We need to stay out of sight even here until we can ride north again. That's all that matters now, that we get out of Mexico and cross the border."

Chapter Sixteen

Run for the Border

A month passed quietly, then a second and a third. Chita's slender, young body began to show a baby bump. At night, standing next to the bed after undressing, she'd take Trey's hand and place it on her stomach while smiling down at him. It moved Trey like nothing else ever had, but he would not admit it aloud. He'd just lay there and smile back at her. He was going to be a father despite himself. He didn't really want to think about what that could mean for both of them and his unborn child. Fight it as he did, he still had wild thoughts. He began to wonder if somehow he and this beautiful Mexican girl he'd taken on the run with him could actually find a place to settle down where no one knew him. It was a dangerous thing even to consider, but it kept coming back.

As both Trey and Chita relaxed, he began walking down to the general store with her to buy food. He always did so cloaked in his bright *serape* and a big sombrero pulled down low over his face. Under the *serape,* his six-gun was tucked in the waistband just in case it was needed.

One Saturday at the store, a dry goods supplier from Guaymas was bringing in sacks of flour over his shoulder one at a time when he noticed the pretty Mexican girl. What caught Manuel Accuna's attention was the tall man standing with her. Although he couldn't get a good look at his face in the shady interior, he could see his nearly shoulder-length hair was almost blond under that big straw sombrero. Back in Guaymas, he's seen wanted posters with a reward for the capture of a gringo murderer and his Mexican girlfriend. He wondered if this pair was possibly them.

Manuel tried not to stare at the couple as he brought in more sacks. When he was finished, the man and woman were walking out the door and he came over to the owner with his bill. "Amigo, do you know who those two are that just left here?" he whispered.

The proprietor glanced up, opened the cash drawer, and shrugged. "No, they live at the top of the hill. They came here maybe three months ago. The man never speaks, only the woman. Why do you ask?"

"For no reason. I just noticed how pretty the young girl is. She carries a child, no?"

"Yes, she does."

"And her husband, is he not a gringo?"

The owner nodded.

"I see. Thank you for your purchase. I will be back next month with more goods. Now I must return to Guaymas. Adios."

When Manuel reached town four days later, he went directly to the police with his suspicions. The officer behind the desk listened intently and then stood, calling for his superior officer in the next room. Minutes later, all three were sitting in Captain Brito's office as Manuel filled in the details.

"There is a reward, is there not?" Manuel asked, looking from man to man.

"Yes," Captain Brito nodded, "If these two you have seen are the gringo and the woman we seek. But first you must come to Pequeño Colina with us to identify them."

Manuel sat back in the chair and his eyes widened. "Will there be shooting?"

"There could be if your claim is correct, but you would not be involved."

"Good." The merchant nodded. "I will go with you. When do we leave?"

"In the morning," the captain answered, "after I get my men together. If you are correct I want these two taken alive so they can stand trial, not killed during the capture. Be back here at six o'clock tomorrow and be ready to ride, my friend. We shall see if you are right or not."

Trey had just gotten up and dressed. The morning sun was beginning to light the houses below when he stepped outside to stretch and yawn. The air was warm and still. The rooster in the yard below began crowing then suddenly stopped mid-cackle. Trey glanced down at the main street. It was empty as usual. Then he noticed a line of saddled horses tied at the hitching post in front of the general store, and he tensed. There weren't that many horses in the entire town, especially with rifle scabbards. He stepped quickly back inside and went over to the bed.

"Chita, get up quick and get our things together. We have to leave now. The police are in town. Hurry, hon!"

Captain Brito spread his men out before ordering them to advance on the cottage above, using houses as a shield. With guns drawn, they edged closer uphill, all eyes fixed on the small structure for some sign of movement. Nothing stirred, as Manuel peeked around the corner of the general store, refusing to move any closer.

Inside the adobe house, Chita hurriedly stuffed the last of their clothes and money into two bulging saddlebags, then ran for the horses tied out back. Trey moved to the front window and peeked downhill. Several policemen came into sight, already nearing the top. Trey lifted his six-gun, steadying it against the window with both hands. When two of the officers edged around the last building into the open, he fired three shots, quickly swinging the pistol from the first officer to the second. Both Mexicans went down kicking and all hell broke loose. Captain Brito's men opened up on the building with rifles and pistols, bullets shattering the hard adobe wall with resounding cracks. Trey stuck his gun around the window again, firing wildly as he emptied his pistol to keep the police from climbing closer. It worked. They all dove for cover as Trey ran out the back door, leaping onto his horse next to Chita who was already in the saddle waiting for him.

"Let's go!" Trey shouted, and they thundered off down the ridge behind the house into tall brush while police stormed the cottage, only to find it empty.

Trey knew he and Chita couldn't take the chance to hole up again. The only option was to run for the border, still hundreds of miles to the north, and run they did. Trey made mental notes to himself each day about things never to do until they safely crossed the Rio Grande. He promised never to spend more than one night in any single place. He vowed not to stay in a Mexican town, regardless of how small or remote. He'd thought they'd be safe in Pequeño Colina, and look what had happened. He thought he and Joshua would be safe living out of La Paz in a fishing village, and Joshua had been killed there. He swore to keep moving, talk to no one, and trust nothing to chance. They had to get clear of Mexico, no matter what.

For the next three weeks they skirted every community they came to, living in the hills and sleeping in their saddle blankets. The farther north they went, the colder the weather became until one night Trey finally relented and built a small fire to keep Chita warm. Long after she went to sleep Trey sat up staring into the dying coals, planning their next move, worried they'd be somehow found out. They were running themselves ragged dodging both the *federales* and the local police. The endless riding and living poorly especially took its toll on Chita. Her vitality, stamina, and physical appearance waned noticeably. Her once sparkling eyes and pretty face were reduced to gaunt lines of fatigue as her stomach grew larger. Once she begged Trey to stop for a few days so that she could rest, but he vehemently refused. Then he realized how desperate she was and apologized, pulling her close, explaining again why they could not take that chance.

They continued north, skirting the towns of El Sueco, Moctezuma, Ahumada, and Samalayuce, as the border drew closer. Finally, one chilly October afternoon they topped a small rise to see the muddy Rio Grande bubbling over a rocky riffle a quarter mile ahead. "We made it, hon. Once we cross, we're safe. Let's get to it," Trey urged, kicking his horse ahead.

Down along the brushy waterway and out of sight, half a dozen Mexican *federales* on patrol had taken a break to water their horses. The patrol was one of several sent to the border when the gringo and his woman had not been found. The *federales'* commander, Vincente Delavega, had spent weeks trying to track down the American and had failed at every turn. As a last ditch effort—and to save his own reputation—he ordered that the patrols ride the border in hopes they might get lucky and run into the fleeing pair trying to cross. Now it seemed that luck had turned the commander's way at last.

One of the officers turned, scanning the low hills at the back of the river as the horses drank. Suddenly, he made out a pair of riders coming straight at him and his men, and he quickly alerted them. The six men tied their horses off and pulled rifles out of their scabbards, running to spread out in a line to intercept the approaching riders. Trey and Chita came closer, still not knowing what was waiting for them just moments ahead.

"I never thought that muddy water could ever look so good," Trey said, turning to Chita, who had his *serape* wrapped around her to keep warm. "Once we cross over, we'll find a town where you can rest and we can get hot food."

"I weel be so happy when we leef Mexico, and we can stop running." Chita clung to the saddle horn as the horses pushed their way through the tall wall of brush just short of the river. The instant they broke out onto the gravely bank a shout rang out. *"Parada!"* The nearest officer stepped from cover, leveling his rifle and motioning for the couple to dismount as the other *federales* ran to assist him.

Trey's hand moved in a blur, his six-gun clearing the holster as two quick shots rang out and the riflemen crumpled to the gravel, pitching facedown.

"Ride for the other side!" Trey shouted to Chita, swinging his horse around and charging the approaching officers, firing as they came on. Another Mexican cried out and fell, then a third as Chita's horse plunged into the water, throwing up fans of spray while charging for the far side. Water geysers erupted around her from bullet hits until she screamed in pain and fell into the water as Trey yanked his horse around to help her.

The remaining *federales* waded into the stream, still firing until Trey felt a white-hot stab of pain smash into his side. He clung to the saddle horn fighting to stay upright, returning fire until he could reach Chita, who was floating facedown in the water. As he pulled her up, bullets continued exploding around them until Trey's horse staggered. Trey savagely kicked it toward the far bank and finally deposited Chita on the sand. He pulled the wounded animal around, charging back across the stream toward the Mexicans, who were working feverishly to reload.

As he reached shore, his six-gun bucked in his hands, with his final two shots spinning another officer into the water. He slammed the empty pistol back in its holster and yanked the rifle out of its scabbard, firing as he rode over the top of the last pair. One straight shot down killed the fifth Mexican with a bullet in the neck. Trey spun the horse back on the remaining man, swinging the rifle like a battle club. The fleshy crunch of solid steel meeting skin and bone sent the last officer spinning into the water, leaving a crimson wake as he floated slowly away downstream.

Bleeding and grimacing with a wave of pain overtaking him, Trey forced his failing horse back across the river until it went down just short of the bank, breathing its last. He unbuckled the saddlebags, then retrieved Chita's horse, staggering to her. He knelt beside her, lifting her in his arms. Her eyes rolled back in her head from a bullet wound in the neck. Shaking her, he begged her to speak, but she could not. The woman he loved was dead, along with his unborn child. Trey cradled her in his arms as tears ran down his face. After all the running and close escapes, it was hard to grasp that it would end like this, finally safe on the American side of the Rio Grande. He didn't know how long he stayed there rocking

Chita in his arms, but finally he stopped. Gently he lifted her onto her horse and climbed on behind her to ride away.

Five miles away, the tiny border town of Rio Vista held a few scattered stores and three rows of houses and shacks along both sides of its dirt main street. At the far end of town stood a small church with a dirty, white steeple sticking straight up into the gray, fall sky. At first Trey didn't recognize the sounds coming from the church, but then he realized it was voices singing inside. It was Sunday, and services were being held. Pulling to a stop in front of it, he got down with Chita in his arms and struggled up the stairs to the front door. He stopped for a moment, taking in a deep breath, then kicked the door open.

When he stepped inside the singing stopped, and every face turned to stare wide-eyed at the bloody stranger with the limp woman in his arms. The preacher stood at the pulpit with a Bible in his hands, frozen with indecision. Then he walked down the aisle toward the tall young man.

"Ah, welcome, stranger. Are you in need of help, or your . . . woman?"

Trey stumbled past him without a word until he reached the altar. Slowly he lowered Chita's body onto it, and the preacher followed him. "My woman . . . believed in your God. I want you to see to it that she's buried the right way, with all the singing and praying. I won't be here to see it, so you have to. Be sure it's done right. I'll pay for it."

Trey started back down the aisle with the preacher by his shoulder, as everyone followed them outside, wondering what would happen next. Trey unbuckled a saddlebag and pulled out a fistful of money, stuffing it into the preacher's shirt pocket. "Now, I'm leaving. You do what I told you to." He grimaced with pain, closing his eyes for a moment while leaning on the horse for support.

"But, mister, you're wounded and bleeding. Let us help you. You can't just ride away like this. You won't make it a mile." The preacher reached out, but Trey pushed his hand away.

"I don't need no help from anyone anymore. You just take care of my woman, and make sure her headstone says *Chita Ovalis . . . and child*. Remember that."

When Trey rode out of Rio Vista that day, he was a changed man in more ways than the bloody gash in his side from a Mexican bullet. He'd seen the only person he'd let himself love killed by men who called themselves the law. Any small chance he thought he had for a life as a husband and father were gone, lying dead back in that church. The law had always stood in his way from the time he was a wild teenage kid. Now the law had guns, and they meant to kill him. The name Trey Wingo would be shouted out in bold black-and-white letters on wanted posters throughout the Southwest, with a $1,000 reward for anyone who pointed the finger at him. Before Trey was done living he vowed to stop more than one of those finger pointers from exposing him. A reckless viciousness began to rule Trey's life to a degree even he had never thought possible. The law had taken away Chita Ovalis, and now anyone with a tin star would have to pay for it.

Chapter Seventeen

Killing Spree

Three fast years passed with Trey always on the move, never staying in one place for long. In Tucson, he robbed a bank in broad daylight, gunning down the guard who ran after him out into the street. In Mesa, he held up a bar and faro house in the wee hours of the morning when the tables were full of cash from the previous night's gambling. Backing out of the door with his sawed-off shotgun, he admonished patrons, who had their hands in the air, that gambling was a sucker's game, and he hoped he'd taught them a lesson. When the barman dove for a weapon under the counter, Trey cut him down with a double blast from the scattergun.

He rode east into New Mexico Territory, holding up the six-horse stage to Las Cruces and demanding the money box under the driver's seat. The shotgun guard made a move to lift up the seat, but instead came up with his own short-barreled .12 gauge. Trey cut him nearly in two with blasts from his double barrel as the guard fell dead between the horses. Then he marched the passengers out, robbing them of all their valuables except for one young woman who was petrified to the

145

verge of tears. Trey's hand clutched the gold necklace on her neck, his mind flashing back to Chita's pretty face. Her memory still haunted him. He slowly lowered his hand and retreated to his horse, mounting up to ride away.

Trey decided to turn north and hide out in the bigger town of Albuquerque for a while to get lost in the crowds. Lawmen were crisscrossing the South trying to find him. He had plenty of cash and needed to lay low to take the heat off him.

For the next two months he holed up in a cheap hotel on the south side of town, going out only at night when he'd be hard to recognize. After eating he'd head back to his room and lay in bed thinking about his life, the murderous path he'd chosen since Chita's death, what to do next and where. His thoughts began to turn toward home, his mother, Samantha, and his brother, Frank. He wondered how they were doing and if they'd heard about him. Maybe, he thought, it might be time to ride north again and go home. At least he'd be away from everyone looking for him here.

When Trey left Albuquerque, he rode along the foothills of the Continental Divide following the White River mountains. Winter was at hand and the cold and first snows made the going slow. Two weeks later he stopped in the small town of Craig to rest his horse and himself for a few days. Ten days later he reached Rawlings, Wyoming Territory, where the weather was even worse. Blowing snow and freezing temperatures took their toll on horse and rider. He stayed for three days then struck out again. In Butte, Montana, he had to buy a new horse. His old mount had given out, and he wasn't very far from doing the same. At least in this part of the country no one recognized him as anything more than a winter traveler bucking what nature threw at him.

At Langley's Stable, the owner, bundled up in heavy

clothes, gloves, and a scarf-tied hat, eyed the whiskered rider as he led out the new horse. "Kinda a bad time of year to be out on the trail, ain't it?"

Trey eyed the older man as he reached into his coat to pay for the animal. "How much?"

Langley pulled at his chin for a moment. "Well, he ain't the prettiest animal I ever saw, but he's big and strong. Right about now I'd say he's worth about forty dollars."

Trey pulled out a roll of bills and paid him off. "Has he been shoed recently? For forty dollars I want a fresh-shoed horse."

"Why yeah, he has. I shoed him myself just two weeks ago. He's ready to go, if you don't both freeze to death. I guess if you mean to ride out in this weather I might as well wish you a Merry Christmas too."

Trey stopped cinching the saddle and looked up at the falling snow drifting down. *Christmas.* He'd almost forgotten the word because he hadn't heard it in years. Langley saw the strange look in his eyes. "When is it?" Trey finally asked, finishing off the saddle.

"Only ten days away. I thought I might as well get in the mood with any customers that come in. So, Merry Christmas to you, stranger!"

Trey didn't answer. He climbed into the saddle and rode out into the falling snow. Maybe he could make it home by the holiday. If he did, it might have some real meaning, at least to his mother and brother. To Trey, it was just another winter day, but the thought of home would keep him riding into the teeth of December gales.

Days on the trail grew longer as chilling winds cut through his clothes like a knife. After another week he skirted Helena, knowing he was closing in on home. He tried not to think about the remaining miles ahead. His gloved hands turned numb, and his feet felt frozen to the stirrups, as snow piled up on the saddle and steam rose from the back of the laboring animal.

One gray evening just before dark he reined to a halt on the banks of a small creek. Bare tree branches were hung with crystal icicles, the little waterway frozen solid from top to bottom, and snow flurries silently spiraled down. Trey's face was covered with a scarf. He pulled the scarf down, his tired eyes studying the scene. Suddenly he realized he was on the banks of his old boyhood playground, Copper Creek. The ranch was less than an hour away. He took in a deep breath, pounded his gloved hands together to restore some feeling, then urged the tired animal forward. "Don't quit on me now," he whispered. "We'll both rest pretty soon."

Inside the Wingo ranch house Samantha had put dinner on the table just as Frank came through the door. He took off his heavy coat to sit down to eat. "You get the horses fed?" she asked.

"Yeah, I've got them all in the barn too. Looks like another big snow tonight. I stacked more wood on the porch too. We'll have to keep this fire going most of the night. The quick in the thermometer outside is frozen in the bottom. Now let's get to some of that hot soup. I'm frozen right down to my socks."

Frank and Samantha were halfway through dinner when they heard muffled footsteps on the porch. He stopped, holding the spoon halfway to his mouth as his mother stared back, eyes questioning. Frank got to his feet, moving to lift the shotgun off its pegs on the wall. He motioned to her to go into the kitchen while he turned to slowly advance on the front door. Leveling the scattergun, he reached for the handle.

"Whoever's out there better start talking, and I mean right now!" Frank barked, turning the handle until it clicked free.

He hesitated a moment to listen. No answer. Slowly he pushed the door open with the shotgun barrel, holding it belt high with both hammers cocked full back and his finger on the trigger.

The light from inside framed a tall man bundled in heavy clothes. He loosened the scarf covering his gaunt face. Ice crystals powdered his hair and eyebrows. As the scarf came down, Frank's eyes widened in disbelief. His mouth opened but no words came out. He stepped forward, wrapping his arms around his brother and pounding him on the back with the shotgun still clutched in one hand. "Trey . . . I . . . we . . . thought you might be dead by now. I can't believe you made it back here alive. Get yourself in here right now!"

"Where's Ma?" Trey's voice was a whisper, as Frank closed the door behind him.

"She's in the kitchen. I'll call her out. Don't move."

"Frank, who is it? Is it okay to come out now?"

"Yes, Ma. It's all right. We've got company. Come see who."

Samantha exited the kitchen, head cocked as she came around the corner facing the door. "Who would come out here on a night like . . ." She stopped dead in her tracks as Trey stepped into full light, taking off his hat and letting his matted hair fall to his shoulders. Her hands went to her mouth and a small cry came. Tears welled up in her eyes as she ran forward, and Trey swept her up in his arms, lifting her off the floor. "Trey! For God's sake I can't believe it's you, after all this time! Oh, Trey, I never stopped praying for you."

"Come on over by the fireplace. You look half-frozen. Give me your coat and hat. We can talk more after you warm up." Frank steered them both toward some chairs in front of the crackling flames dancing in the firepit while Samantha still clung to him, running her hands across his scarred and whiskered face. The luscious heat burned through Trey's wet shirt until steam rose from his back while his mother massaged his neck. For the next hour the questions and answers never stopped, until Trey asked for something hot to eat. After a bowl of soup and a cup of coffee, he continued to talk about his time in Mexico, Porto Oro, and La Paz, and finally told them about Chita's death on the Rio Grande, the child she was carrying, and how rage drove him after that. His mother and brother sat spellbound, listening to it all, hardly interrupting to say a word.

"After the Mexicans killed her, I didn't give a damn about much of anything, including myself or anyone else. I guess I just went sort of crazy. Maybe I still am," Trey admitted.

Samantha moved closer and stroked his long hair as she fought back more tears. "We heard about some of what you said from Johnny Blades," she said, and Trey turned at the mention of Johnny's name. "I guess you don't know about him now, do you?"

"What about him? Is he here?" Trey asked with concern.

"He came back several years ago and turned himself in to the law," Frank interjected. "He did two and a half years in prison down in Helena. Before he went in he married that Mormon girl, Laura. They have a little girl now and live in town."

"Yeah, I remember him telling me he'd do that before I pulled out of Utah." Trey nodded. "I told him he'd be crazy if he did. Looks like he didn't take my word."

"That ain't all. Johnny got himself religion from his new wife. After he got back here he stayed on his folks' ranch for a while, then ran for sheriff after Gibber died. He won too. He's the new lawman down in Loyalton now."

Trey's eyes narrowed, looking from Frank to his mother. "I don't believe it."

"You better. Since he pinned that star on he's rode out here twice in the last year asking if we heard anything from you or where you might be. Naturally, we told him we didn't know anything, because it was only the truth."

"It's a good thing Gibber kicked off on his own. He started all this and if I ran into him now I'd take him down myself." Trey lowered his coffee cup while looking at Frank. "Johnny better not come back here while I'm around. There'd be hell to pay if he does."

Samantha came to Trey's side, the concern obvious on her face. "Trey, you know how much me and your brother wanted you back home with us no matter what you've done. But if Johnny does find out you're here, there'll only be more trouble. Maybe you'd be safer to rest up here for a few days, then find someplace else to move to close by like Eagleville. Frank and I could ride over there every once in a while to see you. I can't stand the thought of you and Johnny facing each other the way things are now."

Trey got to his feet and put both hands on his mother's shoulders. "Listen to me, Ma. I came home because I'm tired of running. I've got no place left to go, and I'm not going to let someone else prod me into running again no matter who it is. I've had a belly full of running. Besides, no one is going to ride out here all the way from town in the middle of winter, so stop worrying about it. I'm home and I'll be here for a long spell. Now I want to get out of these wet clothes and get a real night's sleep. Frank, would you take care of my horse and bring my saddlebags and rifle in too? I need some shut-eye."

"Sure thing. You go ahead and get some rest. I'll tend to your stuff."

Trey was already asleep when his brother came back in with his saddlebags and rifle and laid them on the table. He hefted the heavy leather bags and heard the muffled jingle of coins, then looked up at Samantha. His hands moved, unbuckling each one and pulling the flap back as she came around the table. They both looked in and saw stacks of gold and silver coins. Her hand came to her mouth as she stared back at Frank. Neither said a word, and he buckled the bags back up. Frank walked back across the room, staring into the fire as he rubbed his forehead in concern. At least, he thought, his brother was home for Christmas. What might happen from here on out was something he knew he could do little about.

The next morning the snow had stopped falling and a dazzling winter sun rose over the white-blanketed pine tops. Howard and Rachel Blades carried their Christmas presents to the two-horse sleigh in front of their ranch house. Rachel, bundled up and wrapped tight in a bright red scarf, wore a big smile.

"I know Samantha will be surprised to see us, and so will Frank," Rachel said. "The least we can do is bring them some Christmas cheer after all they've been through, especially that poor woman. Hurry, Howard. I want to get over there as soon as possible. This fresh-baked apple pie will put a smile on her face, I'm sure of it."

"All right, hold your horses, hon." He turned, heading back for the front door. "Just let me grab my rifle in case we run into wolves or something on the way over."

Almost two hours later the sleigh came gliding out of timber as the Wingo ranch came in sight, blue smoke spiraling up from the chimney against the white of the meadow. Frank, out on the front porch, had just stacked a load of firewood in his arms when he looked up to see the sleigh approaching. He quickly dropped the stack and stepped back inside to tell Samantha company was coming. Then he ran for the bedroom to warn Trey too.

"I don't know who it is, but it's not the law, not in a sleigh.

The only people I can think of is the Bladeses. They're the only ones even close. Do you want to duck out the back before they get here?"

"I told you yesterday I'm done running, and I meant it." Trey pulled on his pants and shirt. "Go out and calm Mom down before she's a nervous wreck. You just let me handle it." He glanced at his gun belt on the table next to the bed as Frank exited the room.

When the Bladeses knocked on the front door, Samantha opened it, greeting them with mock enthusiasm and inviting them inside. Frank and Howard shook hands and exchanged Christmas greetings while Rachel took off her heavy coat. Looking around the room for someplace to put it, she noticed the saddlebags on the kitchen table, the rifle laying next to it, and a pair of heavy boots drying out next to the fireplace. Samantha hadn't had time to even think about hiding all of it. Rachel's eyes went around the room, stopping at the partially opened bedroom door, before looking back at Samantha. "Do you have someone visiting? If we'd known you had company, we wouldn't have come over."

Samantha couldn't answer. Words stuck in her throat and fear flashed in her eyes as Frank came to her side, putting his arm around her for support. Before he could speak, the bedroom door slowly creaked open, framing Trey Wingo, who was staring back at the Bladeses.

Chapter Eighteen

Christmas Surprise

Now it was Howard and Rachel who couldn't find the words to speak. They stared at the tall, whiskered man, almost unable to recognize Trey until he spoke. "Yeah, I guess you could say Ma and Frank got company, all right. I've come home, at least for a while." Trey stepped through the door and walked toward the stunned pair until they were face-to-face. Neither of them could believe how much older he looked than his years. Even under a heavy beard the lines on his face were visible and his eyes reflected the coldness of a man who'd seen too much to care anymore. Gone was the devilish smile of a rebellious teenage kid. Howard finally spoke, ending the tension-packed silence.

"Well . . . Trey . . . we wondered what happened to you after all this time. I'm glad to see you're still in one piece. We just came over to wish your mother and Frank a Merry Christmas. We won't stay long. Did you just get back home?"

Trey ignored the question and turned to walk across the room into the kitchen. He poured himself a cup of hot coffee. "How's my old pal, Johnny?" he asked without turning around. "I hear he's turned over a new leaf and got himself a tin star to

154

wear. Imagine that, after all he and I went through together."

"He paid for all that in prison, Trey," Howard was quick to respond. "Besides, Johnny is married and has himself a little girl too. Those days are over for him."

"Yeah, I knew her back in Utah. Pretty girl with big, blue eyes. He was done the first time she looked at him. I told him to be careful, but I guess he didn't listen, huh?"

"He and the family are coming out to our place for Christmas . . ." Rachel trailed off, realizing how awkward she sounded.

Trey walked back across the room while sipping at the coffee until he was facing the Bladeses again. "If you see Johnny it might be smart *not* to tell him I'm here. Now that he's taken up with the law, that wouldn't be the thing to do. Know what I mean?"

Howard and Rachel stood silent. The implied threat was obvious enough. Howard cleared his throat, trying to smooth things over. "Listen, Trey, none of us want any kind of trouble, and that includes our son. And you don't have to worry about us telling anyone you're here, because we won't. Just remember you and Johnny were once close friends, that's all my wife and I are asking. We're going to head back home now. Samantha, Frank, Merry Christmas. You too, Trey."

After they left Frank looked at his brother. "Well, what do you think about Johnny wearing a star?"

"I don't think anything about it. If he doesn't let that badge go to his head, there won't be any trouble. If he does, that's something else again. If I want to go into town I won't let him being there stop me either. I want to be left alone, Frank. That's why I came back home. Not to stir up any more trouble than I'm already packing."

* * *

The next morning Sheriff Blades was sloshing through snow down the boardwalks of Loyalton, bundled in heavy clothes with a wool scarf around his neck, all under a wide-brimmed hat. At just twenty years old, he was the youngest sheriff ever elected, but was still respected and well liked by everyone in town after Gibber's lackluster tenure.

A light snow was falling, adding another ten inches to the already snowy ground. Johnny stopped at Dawsen's dry goods store and pushed the door open, spotting Lem Dawsen feeding kindling into the pot-bellied stove in the center of the room.

"Morning, Sheriff," Lem smiled as the stove crackled. "Looks like a white Christmas for sure, huh?"

"Yes, it does. Tell the missus I said Merry Christmas to her too when she comes to work."

"The same to you, Laura, and the baby. Don't get your feet wet out there. You don't want to be sick Christmas day."

Johnny closed the door and continued down the walkway, greeting other merchants just opening up on Loyalton's four-block-long main street. Finishing the last block, he crossed the street and went into his office. As the door closed, he was unable to see two riders just coming into town, their hats, jackets, and horses covered in several inches of new white. They eyed the SHERIFF'S OFFICE sign hanging over the door as they passed, continuing down the street until reining to a stop in front of the Placer King Hotel at the far end of town.

"Bank's on the corner," Mick George muttered under his breath, peering over the saddle as he untied his saddlebags.

"Yeah, I saw it," Ira Heap answered, his dark eyes darting up and down the street. "One-horse sheriff's office too. He won't be any trouble either. Let's get a room and get out of these wet clothes and warm up. I'm about half froze to death."

After taking a room on the second floor and changing clothes, Mick and Ira exited the hotel, sizing up the town as they walked the boardwalks on both sides of the street. When they reached the bank on the corner both went in, and Mick went to the teller window, feigning questions about opening an account while Ira looked around and located the open safe behind the teller's cage.

"You open tomorrow?" Mick asked.

"Yes, but only until noon. Then we'll close for Christmas the next day. If you'd like to open an account, today would be best to do so." She smiled back.

Mick said he'd have to think about it, and he and Ira exited the bank. "No guard, one teller, and a bank manager at a desk over in the corner," Ira informed him. "You figure they got a gun hid under the counter?"

"Even if they did, that woman ain't going to go for it. I say the whole place looks like easy pickins to me. We'll clean it out when they open, lock them two in the safe, and be down the road before anyone knows the difference. This is going to be sweet, easy, and quick."

The pair went back to the hotel, resolved not to go out drinking and suffer a case of whisky mouth or a drunken stupor that would leave them unable to take the bank. Mick stretched out on the bed, slowly clicking the cylinders of his six-gun while checking each one to be certain it was full. Ira pulled a chair to the window and sat leaning back, watching the street below, passing time. Both men savored the thought of taking the bank so easily. These one-horse mountain towns in Montana were all the same, Mick thought to himself. No one ever gave a thought to a real stickup. That only happened in the bigger towns. Ira stiffened in the chair, getting to his feet to press his face against the window.

"Hey, Mick. Come take a look at this. There's the local law down there and he's all alone, don't even have a deputy."

Mick came to the window and watched Johnny Blades walking down the snowy boardwalk below. "Like I said, it's gonna be sweet and quick." He went back to the bed, stretching out as a slow grin lit his whiskered face.

The next morning a bitter wind was spitting snow again. Johnny finished his breakfast, strapped on his gun belt, then pulled on a heavy jacket, hat, and gloves. "Are you going to be home early?" Laura asked.

"Maybe, hon. I think everyone is going to close after lunch, so I just might. Tomorrow we can hitch up the sleigh and head out to see Ma and Pa. I hope this snow doesn't get too bad by then." He leaned close and kissed Laura on the cheek. "Keep Carrie inside today. If you need anything at the store, I'll pick it up after I lock up the office. Don't go outside."

Laura walked him to the door. One quick hug and he was out. She stood watching him trudge through the snow toward the main street two blocks away. She loved Johnny so much it almost scared her to see him leave every day, worrying about him. Her only solace was that she knew Johnny didn't push the law by cracking heads or pulling his gun. He always tried to reason with folks, and in quiet Loyalton, that was appreciated by everyone. That's why he'd won the job in the first place. Townspeople had had enough of George Gibber and his ways to want a change. In Johnny Blades, they got a big one.

Mick George and Ira Heap came downstairs into the hotel lobby, checking the clicking wall clock over the clerk's desk. Eight-forty-five. The bank would be open in fifteen minutes. Mick paid for the room, and they went down to the livery stable to pay Ladd too. After tying on their saddlebags, both rode back down the street to the bank. Dismounting, they pulled up their coat collars, checked the street both ways, and stepped up onto the boardwalk. Right on time the gray-haired bank owner, Joseph Sinclair, came walking quickly toward them until he stopped to unlock the front door.

"Good morning, gentlemen," the bank owner nodded. "We'll be open in just a few minutes after Mrs. Leland arrives. We won't keep you waiting out here in the cold any longer than necessary."

"We know you won't." Ira shoved his .45 hard against Joseph's ribs, cocking the hammer with a cold click. "Now get that damn door open and I mean right quick!"

Mr. Sinclair's eyes widened in alarm as he fumbled for the keys with gloved hands in his coat pocket. He inserted the keys into the lock until the door creaked open and he was shoved inside. Mick quickly pulled the shade down while Ira steered the old man toward the wall safe.

"Open it and fast!" he ordered, moving the pistol up under Mr. Sinclair's ear, while Mick pulled the shade back just far enough to see Mrs. Leland approaching the front door. She started to reach for the handle but was startled when Mick yanked it open and pulled her inside, threatening her to keep quiet as he pushed her into a sitting position on the floor. He quickly tied her hands behind her back, shoving his dirty bandana in her mouth as she gagged on it.

Mr. Sinclair's trembling hands turned the safe dial combination but the big door wouldn't budge, enraging Ira, who spun him around and smashed his head against the steel door. "You get it open this time, or I'll blow your liver out on the floor, you understand!"

With blood running down his face, the old man tried to calm himself, slowly working the dial again. "What's taking so long?" Mick called from outside the teller's cage, as he peeked outside again to check the sidewalk and street. Suddenly he stiffened. A lone figure appeared walking toward the bank, wearing a tin star just visible under his unbuttoned coat. "Here comes the law. Better get that cash and quick, or we'll hafta shoot our way out of here!"

The safe door finally swung open, and Ira shoved the bank owner inside, ordering him to fill with cash two large canvas bags he pulled from his coat. "No paper. Only gold and silver coins!" he hissed, glancing toward Mick at the door. The old man began filling the sacks, and Mick pulled Mrs. Leland to her feet, hustling her into the vault. When the sacks were filled, Ira tied Mr. Sinclair's hands and feet and stuffed a gag in his mouth too, ordering both of them down on the floor. Stepping outside the vault, the pair pushed the steel door shut and spun the lock handle, just as Johnny Blades tried the front door handle of the bank.

Surprised that the bank was still closed, he tried knocking on the door, putting his gloved hands to the glass to try to see around the shade.

"Is there another way out of here?" Ira whispered. Both men looked around, seeing a second door down a narrow hallway.

"Let's try it." Mick nodded. At the door they twisted the dead-bolt lock and stepped out into an alley with guns in their hands. Up against the brick wall, Mick and Ira eased their way back around to the main street, where Johnny, his back to the pair, was still knocking, calling out for Mr. Sinclair to open the door.

"You!" Ira called out as Johnny turned, facing two six-guns leveled at his stomach fifteen feet away. "Get away from that door and get back in the alley. Move or I'll drop you where you stand!"

Johnny stepped away, lifting his hands slightly. "Keep your

damn hands down," Mick hissed under his breath, "and get over here."

"Where's your hog leg?" Mick asked. Johnny unbuttoned his coat until the weapon became visible. "Two fingers. Lift it out and throw it on the ground. Ira, you get the horses and bring them around here." He turned back to Johnny. "Mister, you showed up at the wrong time, and that's going to cost you. Get up against that wall and say your prayers."

None of them noticed a rider coming down the street through the falling snow, halting then dismounting while studying the three men just visible at the entrance to the alley. Was that the dull flash of a badge? Trey squinted, trying to make it out. The two men with their backs to him looked like they were leveling pistols. Snow crunching under his boots, he started forward as he opened his coat, clearing his six-gun. Johnny saw the shadowed form of a man looming through the curtain of falling snow.

"You boys ain't up to no good, are you!" Trey's husky voice cut through the storm like a knife, his hand already on his wheel gun as Ira and Mick spun around at the sudden intrusion. Before either could fire, Trey's wheel gun spit three spears of flame in quick succession, and the pair went down rolling in the snow without getting off a single shot, as Johnny dove out of the line of fire.

The sheriff got back on his feet and stepped closer until he got a clear look at the gunman's drawn and whiskered face. Johnny couldn't believe his eyes even now. His mouth opened to say something but the words got stuck in his throat. He tried again. "Trey . . . is that . . . you? I never thought I'd see you alive again, and certainly not here in Loyalton."

Trey holstered his pistol and a grim smile came over his face. "The world *is* full of surprises, ain't it, Johnny?"

Chapter Nineteen

Desperados

After the bodies were taken away and Johnny ordered the crowd that had gathered to disperse, he asked Trey to follow him back to his office for a talk. Johnny was already struggling with what to say and how to say it, but he knew if he didn't say something he never would. When they stepped inside, Trey made sure Johnny went first. He wasn't going to let anyone wearing a tin star get behind him, even his old boyhood pal. Johnny shucked out of his coat, unbuckling his gun belt and hanging it on a wall peg next to a gun rack.

Trey kept his gun belt on. Johnny went to the potbellied stove over in the corner and fed it fresh kindling. Then he lit a match to warm the ice-cold room as Trey stood watching him intently.

"Sit down for a minute." Johnny nodded toward a chair in front of his desk as he came back to sit. "I guess there's some things we have to talk about."

"Like what?" Trey asked, pulling the chair up and easing into it as the stove began popping to life.

"Well, for starters, the fact that there's paper on you from all over the Southwest. I've got enough of it right here in the office to wallpaper a kitchen, so what are doing back here of all places?"

"I have a ranch and a mother and brother, remember? I figured it was time I came back home and settled down for a while."

"Settled down? After four years and what you've done? These wanted posters say you've killed four men and robbed numerous banks, a stage, and businesses. Do you think the law is just going to forget that and let you go back to raising horses and cattle?"

"Actually, I think it's six men, but I stopped counting some time back. I've been busy since we parted company in Utah and you got religion over that little Mormon gal. That was back when we were *both* desperados." Trey's mouth turned up in a small smile that vanished just as quickly.

Johnny leaned back in the chair, staring at Trey while remembering Utah. "I married her, Trey. And now we have a little girl. If you want to call that religion, go ahead."

"Yeah, I know. Mom and Frank told me you were a regular family man now, being sheriff and all. How do you do that, just forget everything else and pin on a star?"

Johnny's jaw tightened. Now they were getting down to it. He had to say it. "You know you can't stay here, don't you? If I don't take you in someone else will. It's just a matter of time. Why push it? I don't want to have to put a gun on you."

Trey straightened up, his hand slowly moving down until it rested on his pistol. He stared back at Johnny without blinking. "I've been gone four years, like you said, maybe even a little bit more. It was time I came back home. I'm done running.

If the law wants to track me down here, let 'em. At least we'll have it out on my home grounds and not theirs in some po-dunk hole-in-the-wall with a weed-filled boneyard up on a hill."

Johnny swallowed, measuring his words. "Well, just remember I'm the law too, Trey. And I'm sworn to uphold the law against anyone who breaks it. I don't want no trouble between you and me, you know that. But you can't stay here, and that's all there is to it. If I let you slide, folks around here would think I'm no better than Gibber, and I'd have to take this badge off and toss it on the desk. I won't do that. Not even for you, as close as we once were."

Trey got to his feet and put both hands on the desk, his face a grim mask as he leaned forward nearly nose to nose with Johnny. "You think you're the law? Were you the law the night you pulled the trigger in Eagleville, backing me up? Do you re-member three men were killed, and you were right in the thick of it too? You think that tin star you've got pinned on your chest makes you high and mighty, and all that's just forgotten now? You ran from the law just like I did, and all the way to Utah. Don't push your luck with me, Johnny. You can't win, and you know it. I don't want to kill you, but I will if you try anything. I'm telling you this just one time, so you'd better listen up!"

Johnny pulled back in his chair, his eyes still locked on Trey. "I served my time for those killings. I paid my debt to society. You ought to think about doing the same. Maybe if you turned yourself in and explained Kip's murder, they would let you serve time and get out, just like I did."

"Don't make me laugh. The first thing they'd do is measure me for a rope, and you know it!" Trey straightened up, walked to the door, and unlocked it, turning around. "One other thing before I go. You can tell Laura that her brother is dead. The

Mexicans killed him down in La Paz. I don't plan on letting *any* law do the same thing to me."

The door closed and Johnny got to his feet. He went to the window, staring outside at Trey's figure being swallowed up by big, cereal-size snowflakes silently cascading down as he crossed the street. The sheriff hooked his thumbs in his pockets, letting out a deep sigh. This was going to be one Christmas he'd never forget, if he lived long enough to see another one.

Trey made the long, cold ride back home. After arriving he said little to either Frank or his mother about it. His grim attitude said enough, and Frank knew he must have run into Johnny Blades. It was Christmas Eve and Samantha had cooked a big venison roast with all the trimmings. She even baked a crab apple pie for dessert. When they sat down to eat she began a prayer, reaching out to hold both sons' hands.

"I want to thank the Lord for my family being whole again." She stopped, the emotion being almost too much, then caught herself. "I only wish my husband, Kip, could be here to share it with us. Amen."

Frank shot a quick glance across the table at Trey. He was already staring back at him. Kip was cold in his grave, and both of them knew how his murder had changed everyone's lives, especially Trey's. "Let's eat, Mom." Frank broke the uncomfortable silence. "This looks like some kind of feed. You really outdid yourself tonight."

"Merry Christmas, Trey, and you too, Frank. This is the best Christmas I can remember in years, having both my boys here. I'm just so happy."

Later that evening, when the brothers went out on the front porch to get an armload of firewood, Frank immediately questioned Trey about what had happened in town.

"I rode in to get Ma something special for Christmas. I'll give it to her in the morning."

"Okay, but what about Johnny Blades? Did you run into him or not?"

"Yeah, I saw him. He was about to get himself shot down by a couple of bank robbers until I took care of them. Even after I saved his neck he still says I'll have to clear out."

"So what are you going to do?"

"You don't see me packing, do you? I told Johnny not to show up out here or I'd take him down too. He says if I come back to town, he'll try to arrest me. I guess right now it's a Mexican standoff, but it won't last. I've been halfway around the world, and no one is going to tell me where I can and can't go. That includes Johnny. I don't give a damn about anything or anyone except you and Ma."

"If it comes to a gunfight, I'll stand with you!" Frank shot back. "I wasn't there for you last time, but I will be now."

"No, Frank. Someone has to stay here and take care of Ma. You're the one for that, just like you have been while I've been gone. Anything that comes my way, I'll handle it."

Christmas came and went. The snow continued piling up while the Wingo family stayed close to home, taking care of the cattle and horses. They could not know that Sheriff Lawrence Todd, from Eagleville, had written a letter to Johnny Blades saying he'd heard from riders passing through his town that Trey Wingo, the notorious robber and murderer, might be holing up somewhere near Loyalton. He wanted to know if Johnny knew anything about it, or if it was just a rumor. Johnny wanted to handle the tricky business of Trey. He'd hoped he could persuade Trey to either stay a short time and move on or possibly even turn himself in. Now he was being forced to play a different hand. He didn't relish the thought of strangers getting involved, especially more law. That could only lead to more trouble, maybe even a showdown.

Johnny leaned back in his office chair, still uncertain how to answer Sheriff Todd's letter. He finally decided to say he'd only heard the same thing, but hadn't actually seen Trey. Maybe that would satisfy Sheriff Todd not to pursue the subject further.

A week later, after reading the letter, the Eagleville sheriff thought it odd that Loyalton's own sheriff would not know for sure if someone like Trey was in his part of the country, especially after the two businessmen from Loyalton had already informed him of it. Sheriff Todd pulled the wanted poster out of his desk drawer and read it again. TREY WINGO IS WANTED FOR BANK ROBBERY, STAGE HOLDUPS, AND MURDER. REWARD $1,000 LEADING TO HIS ARREST AND CAPTURE.

Sheriff Todd knew if he could get his hands on the fugitive, he'd also solve the nighttime murders of three wanted men four years back in his own town. It would erase the only stain on his otherwise spotless record as sheriff.

The next morning he called in his two deputies, Henry Morgan and James Pace. "Henry, I want you to watch over things here while Jim and I ride over to Loyalton. I'm not sure how long we'll be gone, maybe a week or more, but I know you can handle it until we get back. We'll leave in the morning, so both of you show up early. It's a long ride through the snow. I want to get an early start on it."

"Does this mean after I make my rounds I can sit at your desk and put my feet up on it like you do?" Henry joked, a slow grin spreading across his face.

"Only if no one sees you doing it. You don't want to ruin my good reputation, do you?" All three men laughed.

The pair of lawmen left in the dark the next morning, pushing their horses through deep snow. They arrived in Loyalton past midnight and stayed at the hotel until Johnny arrived the next morning to open up the sheriff's office. He'd barely got a good fire going in the stove when Sheriff Todd and Deputy Pace walked through the door, stomping snow off their boots. Johnny and Sheriff Todd knew each other from Johnny's trial several years earlier, but neither had seen each other since. As they shook hands and Todd introduced his deputy, Johnny's face continued to show surprise.

"Well, Sheriff. What are you doing riding way up here in this kind of weather?" Johnny was first to speak, wondering to himself why Sheriff Todd hadn't let him know he was coming. They walked to the stove to warm their hands, and Sheriff Todd slid off his gloves while eyeing his younger counterpart. Lawrence Todd was in his mid-fifties, tall, slender, with black hair graying at the temples and a well-trimmed mustache. He was the perfect picture of a steely-eyed lawman who didn't stand for any nonsense from anyone. Johnny, on the other hand, was young enough to be his son. It was his first time at wearing a star, and someone Lawrence already considered too inexperienced and not really up to the job.

"From what I hear, it seems pretty clear to me that this Trey Wingo is around here someplace holing up. If that's so, I'd say the three of us have a pretty good chance of finding him and bringing him in. He's wanted for just about everything in the book. If we collar him we'll have done a lot of good for a lot of people, not to mention the thousand-dollar reward that goes with it. We do that, and I'll split it three ways." Sheriff Todd stared at Johnny without blinking.

"Wait a minute," Johnny shot back. "You try that and some-one is going to get killed. Trey is not going to walk in here and give himself up. I know him like neither of you do. You can't crowd him without a gunfight. He's got nothing left to lose, and he knows it. That makes him even more dangerous now."

Sheriff Todd's eyes narrowed. "We're the *law*, for God's sake. I don't give a damn who feels crowded and who does not. We've got a job to do, and no one else is going to do it. I don't care how fast Wingo is either. He can't take on all three of us at the same time and come out on top. Why are you so concerned about him?"

"It's a little hard to explain." Johnny walked over to the desk and sat down. "We were boyhood pals. We did every-thing together, school, hunting, sometimes raising a little hell. Our families are friends too. All this started because his father was robbed and murdered some years back right here in town. Our sheriff wouldn't do anything about it, so Trey decided to do it himself and I went with him. You know how that turned out. I imagine he's staying at their ranch east of here. I can send a message asking him to come into town. Maybe I can try talking him into going on trial. I don't know for sure, but I can try. I don't want to bring him in and then ambush him. I won't be a party to that, I'll tell both of you that right now."

Lawrence glanced at his deputy. The look on his face said more than words, as the sheriff pretended to go along with Johnny's idea. "All right, get hold of him and see what he has to say. But I think you'd be wise not to mention that me and Jim are here too. That might scare him off. It's your call. Go ahead and make it, Sheriff."

Sheriff Todd and James Pace left the office and walked down the boardwalk. The sheriff turned to his deputy with a grim smile. "If this Trey Wingo thinks he's going to ride in here and barter with Blades, he's got another thing coming. I'll cut him down faster than it takes to tell it!"

"Not if I beat you to it." Pace smiled back.

Chapter Twenty

Dreamland

T hree days later, while Trey and Frank were out feeding cattle in the upper pasture, Trey glanced down toward the ranch house to see a rider approaching.

"Who would be riding out here in the middle of winter?" Frank squinted, following his brother's gaze.

"I don't know. I don't recognize the horse or rider either. Let's get back down there before he reaches the house. I don't want Ma having to talk to anyone from town, if that's where he's from."

They trotted their horses downhill through fresh snow, reining to a halt at the hitching post, but staying in the saddle as the stranger rode in. Out of habit Trey's hand moved down to his six-gun, just in case it proved to be trouble.

"How do." The scruffy rider raised a gloved hand, his icy beard a sure sign he'd been riding a long way in this freezing weather. "Name's Cletus Hobb, from Loyalton. Sheriff Blades sent me way out here to deliver this here letter. Either one of you boys named Trey Wingo?"

"I'm Wingo," Trey said, reaching out to take the envelope

but not opening it. "You can tell Blades you done your job when you get back to town. Adios."

Hobb rubbed his unruly beard. "Well, I was kinda hopin' maybe after riding all this way out here and nearly freezing to death, you might offer me a hot drink and a little time to thaw out before I have to start back."

"We don't run no roadhouse. You done your job and likely got paid for it. It's best you just turn that horse around and start back now." Frank's answer was short and quick.

"You mean . . . you're not even going to let me rest for a while? I'm half froze to death!" He lifted his hands, palms up, almost begging and looking from brother to brother.

"You heard Frank!" Trey's voice was louder. "Head on outta here. We don't want no visitors."

After Hobb left, the Wingos went into the house. Trey shucked out of his heavy jacket and walked to the warming flames crackling in the fireplace. He opened the letter, reading it to himself while Frank and Samantha stood quietly watching.

Trey,

Word of your arrival back home is spreading. Before other lawmen try to find and arrest you, I think it's best you come back into town and we talk. I believe we can work out something if you'll try. I know you don't want any trouble showing up at the ranch with your mom and Frank there.

Johnny

Trey handed the letter to his mother while Frank leaned over her shoulder and they both read it. Samantha's face immediately grew tense with fear. "Don't go into Loyalton, Trey. Just stay here where you're safe. Please don't, Son."

"Mom's right," Frank cut in. "In town there's no telling what might happen. Let Blades come out here, if he wants to talk. You goin' in there don't make any sense. Maybe it's a trap or something?"

Trey walked over into the kitchen and poured himself a hot cup of coffee without saying a word. He went to the window, looking out at the snowy landscape sparkling like a million diamonds under the dazzling winter sun. "I'll think on it." Both Samantha and Frank knew that was the end of the conversation, whether they liked it or not.

That night Trey lay in bed long after his mother and brother were asleep. He stared up at the shadowy timber beams he, his father, and Frank had erected so long ago. The icy December full moon outside reflecting off the snow made them almost glow in the dark.

Johnny's letter kept him awake. He remembered back when they were both just kids, palling around together, hunting, fishing, going to school, racing their horses, literally growing up together. He remembered all the trouble he got into and Johnny following him into it. Now maybe there was an end in sight. What end, he couldn't be sure, but Johnny's letter made more sense than he wanted to admit to himself. He couldn't run forever, and he was certain he didn't want a shootout here at the ranch with his mother and brother in jeopardy. Maybe the time had come to consider trying something else, whatever Johnny suggested.

Long before dawn Trey was up, dressed, and strapping on his gun belt. He slipped into a heavy coat and gloves, scribbling a short note that he left on the kitchen table. Out in the barn he saddled his horse, pulling himself up into the cold, squeaky saddle. Once out of the barn, he pulled to a brief stop to look at the ranch house covered in white snow under the glow of the moon. He wondered if he'd ever see it again and his mother and brother too. He pulled his horse around, starting for Loyalton. This time he didn't look back.

Trey reached town late that night, pulling to a stop in front of the hotel. Once inside, he rang the bell and a sleepy desk clerk came out of the back room behind the counter, rubbing himself awake. His eyes cleared as he stared back at the late-night customer. Suddenly, he realized who he was facing but tried not to make it obvious.

"I want a room on the second floor. You got one?" Trey asked.

"Ah, yes sir, I do. Room thirteen got cleaned tonight. It's available. But if you don't like that number . . ."

"It'll do. When does the sheriff's office open?"

"Well, sir, generally about eight o'clock in the morning. Sheriff's been pretty popular lately. I got two other guests here who are lawmen coming and going too. I think they're from Eagleville."

Trey stared hard at the clerk. "Lawmen? Are you sure about that?"

"I am. They're both wearing badges, so I guess they must be."

Trey pushed a five-dollar gold piece across the counter. "This is for you to keep quiet about me being here, you understand? If I found out different, I'd have to come in here and take it back. You wouldn't want me to do that, would you?"

"Oh, no sir, I surely wouldn't. Your secret is safe with me. You can count on that. I don't want no trouble of any kind. I'm a peaceable man."

"What room are these lawmen in?"

"Ah, room five, that's right here on the first floor."

Trey turned and went up the stairs to his room. Once inside, he locked the door and checked his pocket watch. Three-fif-teen. After shucking out of his heavy jacket and hat, he laid down on the bed, pulling his six-gun from its holster and slowly rotating the cylinders one click at a time. He checked all six dull, gray slugs snug in their chambers. He thought about Johnny Blades and their meeting just a few hours away. Was Johnny go-ing to offer him some kind of a deal, or would he be foolish enough to actually try and take him in?

Maybe he could do some prison time. He was still a young man of twenty-one. Even if he did five or ten years in prison, he'd still get out a relatively young man with most of his life ahead of him. He could go back to the ranch and make a go of it with his mother and brother. The more he thought about it, the more plausible it seemed, even though he'd said he'd never do time behind bars, no matter what.

If only Kip were here to help tell him what to do, it would all be so much easier. He'd always looked up to his dad, even though he never lived up to his expectations. He just didn't have Kip's temperament and steadfast insistence on doing things the right way, the legal way. Kip had tried to drill that into his head since childhood, but Trey had always been the rebel child, the one who fought against authority, the one who always got into trouble and got whipped for it. Trey stretched out on the bed, remembering his dad and how he'd gotten into his life of crime after his father was gunned down. He closed his eyes and slowly drifted off into a fitful sleep.

Trey rolled listlessly in the bed until dreamland took over. Suddenly he saw Kip walking slowly toward him, his hand raised in hello as he came closer. Trey tried to call to him, but no words came out. Kip came to a stop, staring deep into his son's eyes and putting both hands on Trey's shoulders. Trey could see two bloody bullet holes in his father's shirt, yet Kip showed no sign of pain. Kip began talking in a strangely hollow voice as if he were far away.

"Go back home, son. Do not stay here in town. Go back to your mother and Frank. Do you understand me?"

Trey shook his head to say he didn't understand, and he didn't want to go back home yet, but his mouth seemed locked shut. He tried to reach out and touch his father but his arms were frozen at his side too.

"Do as I've said, Trey. Leave here now. I'm your father . . . there is still time."

Kip's image began drifting back without moving his feet. Trey tried again to reach out and stop him. He didn't want him to go—there was so much he had to ask—but Kip slowly faded away. Trey jerked straight up in the bed, beads of sweat covering his face, as he sucked in a deep breath. He began rubbing the back of his neck with both hands, trying to work out the knots. When he looked up, he realized the room was lit with dawn. Once on his feet, he crossed the room to the window. Snowflakes were spiraling down again. He pulled out his pocket watch: seven-forty-five. If he was going to meet Johnny, he wanted to do it early, first thing, not later when townspeople would be out and about and able to recognize him. Johnny had already told him there was talk he was back in the area. Why feed it by showing himself? He shucked into his heavy coat, checked his six-gun one more time, then pulled the wide-brimmed Stetson down on his head as he walked out the door and down the staircase.

The desk clerk nodded good morning as he passed and pushed through the front door. The icy bite of winter stung Trey's cheeks as he strode down the slushy boardwalk toward the sheriff's office. Once there he started to knock, but decided to just walk straight in. Johnny was at the potbellied stove with his back to the door when Trey entered.

"Trey," Johnny said as he straightened up. "I'm real glad you decided to come in. It saves a lot of trouble all the way around. I'll have a pot of coffee boiling pretty quick. Sit down. Let's talk."

"Go ahead, Johnny. You're the one who asked me here. You do all the talking."

Johnny came over to the desk and sat down, explaining that out-of-town lawmen were already in town, suspicious that he was in the area. He promised Trey that if he turned himself in to him, he'd stand up for him in court when he faced charges. "We both know how your dad was killed and what that led to. The court has to take that into account, especially with me testifying on your behalf. I did my time for my part in it, and I think there's a good chance you could too, instead of running for the rest of your life with a price on your head. Think about it, Trey. This is the best chance you'll ever have."

Trey stared back across the desk at his old boyhood pal. Even as a kid Johnny was always the trusting one. But this time could he be right? Was there a chance he could stop running? It almost sounded too good to be true. Trey pulled at his chin, never taking his eyes off Johnny. "And what about Mexico?" he asked. "You think the law is just going to forget about my time down there, and my battles with the *federales*? I've never even told you about that and what I got into."

"What happened after you left Utah with Joshua isn't what you're being charged with now. The killings in Eagleville are the main charge. That's all you'll have to face."

"After I crossed the Rio Grande and came back, I knocked

off a couple of banks and stages down south. There was gun-play and blood was shed. You gonna fix that up too?"

Johnny leaned back in his chair and folded his arms across his chest as he thought it over. The stove began to pop and the coffeepot boiled. He got to his feet, fetching two cups off the rack. "If I remember right, you take your coffee black."

Trey nodded as Johnny came back to the desk, pushing the cup across the top. He lifted the steaming liquid and took a small sip. "I had a dream last night."

Johnny looked up, wondering why he'd mention something like that.

"I saw my dad. He told me to clear out of town. He said I was heading for trouble if I stayed. Am I, Johnny?"

Johnny stared back and the look on his face answered the question. "I won't lie to you, Trey. There are two lawmen who rode in here from Eagleville a couple of days ago asking questions about you. That's the main reason I wrote you in the first place. To get you in here and under custody before some-one put a bullet in your back, whether it is the law or someone just looking to collect the reward. The safest place you can be right now is here locked up in my jail, even if you don't think so. You've got to understand that. Out on the street or at your ranch you're fair game for anyone."

"Yeah, and if I do what you want I'd be fair game for the hangman too." Trey eased out of the chair looking down at his old friend. "I said a long time ago I'd never end up behind bars, that I'd rather die first. But I'll give you this much. If you can make a deal in writing with the territorial governor that I do just a few years' time then have all charges against me dropped, I'll consider what you're saying. I'll be out at the ranch when you get an answer."

Trey put down the cup and turned, starting for the door. For just a fleeting instant Johnny had the drop on him. All he had to do was pull his six-gun and stop him right where he stood. But he couldn't do it. Instead, he let out a slow breath and promised Trey he'd get an answer to him as quick as he could. Trey turned back. "I know you're trying to help, but it's got to be my way or no way. That's just the way it is. I don't want to go up against you, Johnny, because you wouldn't stand a chance. You just better do the best you can, while you can."

Over in the lobby of the Placer King Hotel, Sheriff Todd and his deputy had just come downstairs when the desk clerk called them over while looking out the front window to be sure Trey wasn't in sight. "As a good citizen I think I should tell both of you that Trey Wingo is over at the sheriff's office right now."

"And how do you know that?" Todd questioned skeptically.

"Because he just walked out of here fifteen minutes ago. He paid me not to tell anyone he stayed here last night, but a killer like that shouldn't be on the loose. If you capture him, re-member about the reward money. I'm the one who turned him in. I'd be entitled to it, wouldn't I?"

Sheriff Todd turned to Deputy Pace. "Get upstairs and get the shotgun and rifle out of our room. Then get back down here double quick! And you," he turned to the clerk, "better get out of sight in case there's gunplay. If it is Trey Wingo, he's not just going to lay down and give it up."

Chapter Twenty-one

Showdown in the Snow

Johnny got up, meeting Trey at the door. "Just don't do anything reckless until I have an answer from the people down in Helena. It might take a little while to get it."

"I'm heading back to the ranch. There isn't much to get wild about out there."

"And tell your mom and Frank I send my best to both of them. They're good people." Johnny stuck out his hand and Trey took it, both shaking hard, staring each other in the eye without blinking. Trey turned, pulled up his coat collar, and stepped outside. The wind was rising, blowing big, nickel-size flakes around as he started down the boardwalk.

Johnny went to the window, watching Trey step off the boardwalk and cross the snowy street. He wondered if it was possible his plan would work. If it didn't, he knew what the consequences would be. He'd have to try and take Trey by himself, and that would be plain suicide. That's when Johnny noticed the dim outline of a man on the opposite boardwalk behind the curtain of falling snow. It looked like the man had a shotgun in his hands. He rushed to the door, stepping outside just in time to hear a voice call out, "This is Sheriff Todd from Eagleville. You're under arrest. Open your coat and throw down your hog leg. Do it now or we'll cut you down where you stand!"

Trey stopped in midstride, eyes staring at the figure, when a second voice cut the icy air. "We've got you double-covered, Wingo," Deputy Pace called out while leveling his rifle from Johnny's side of the street. "Better do what Sheriff Todd says, and I mean right now, or you're a dead man!"

"Wait," Johnny called out, stepping into the street and waving both hands. "This man is under my custody. Put your guns down!"

"Not a chance!" Todd yelled back. "You could have locked him up and you didn't. Now he's going behind bars in my town. You step back out of it. Jim, get his pistol while I cover him!"

Deputy Pace stepped off the porch, still leveling his rifle as Trey unbuttoned his coat. The instant his holster was in the clear Trey pulled his six-gun, crouching to steady himself and firing three lightning-fast shots. The deputy screamed as he fell face-first into the snow, pulling off a wild rifle shot as he went down. Sheriff Todd's scattergun belched smoke and flame, sending a volley of buckshot cutting into Trey, who went down, rolling in the snow. Then Trey double-handed his pistol, emptying the final three shots and driving Sheriff Todd back through a storefront window, mortally wounded.

Johnny ran to Trey laying on his back in the snow, a small trickle of blood oozing out the side of his mouth as he stared up into falling snowflakes. "I didn't know they were going to do this, Trey, I swear to Christ I didn't. You've got to believe me!"

Trey's eyes flickered as his chest rose and fell, struggling to draw a breath. Only a sickening rattle of death came out. Johnny carefully lifted him, cradling him in his arms as tears welled up in his eyes. Trey's right hand slowly lifted, grabbing the young sheriff by his shirt. His eyes closed a moment then opened again as he tried with everything he had to speak. "Tell . . . Ma . . . and Frank . . . I didn't mean for it . . . to end like this. Tell them . . . I want to be . . . buried back at . . . the ranch . . . not here in this . . . damn town."

Several storekeepers came outside, running toward the pair. "Get the doctor, get him quick!" Johnny yelled.

"I . . . don't need no . . . doctor. I'm going to see . . . Pa . . . just like in my . . . dream. It's been one hell of a ride . . . hasn't it, Johnny?" Trey's hand fell away, and his eyes closed for the last time. There in the snow Johnny Blades began sobbing quietly as he held his old friend.

Trey was buried in the high meadow behind the ranch where his stone cross could be seen from the kitchen window by Samantha. She insisted on the cross, even though the only church her son ever walked into that she knew of was the one just across the border where he carried the body of Chita Ovalis to be buried. Johnny spoke the eulogy at the burial, struggling to even finish the short ten minutes. Mostly, he recalled their boyhood years together, the fun times, playing hooky from school and the mischief they got into, Trey's insatiable desire for adventure and his rambunctious struggle against authority. The crime-ridden days were left out in deference to Samantha, who looked like she'd aged ten years overnight. Frank physically supported his mother throughout the service, his stony face frozen in pain. He simply stared off at the snowy high country around them all. He could not bring himself to look down at the pine coffin in which his beloved brother lay.

As for Johnny, Trey's death affected him greatly too. He gave up his position as sheriff, turning in his badge shortly after the service. He'd lost his respect for the job and the laws he'd been sworn to uphold after the ambush and shootout on the street. Instead, he moved out of Loyalton back to his mother and father's ranch along with his young family, to build a second log home next to his folks. He would go into partnership with his dad, raising cattle and horses in Big Sky Country, and return to the simpler life he'd always loved. Maybe, in some way, his original run for sheriff had really only been his way of redeeming his name and reputation after the killings in Eagleville years earlier. Now none of that seemed to matter anymore.

When spring lit the sky again in the pine-studded high country and winter snows melted away to be replaced by blossoming wildflowers, Johnny would ride out alone, checking on the cattle. He would rein to a halt on a high ridge above the ranch, where he could see the twinkling dance of Copper Creek rushing away in a canyon far below.

Suddenly the same old memory would return of he and Trey wildly racing each other bareback home from school to see who would be first to reach the riffles at the ford, watching the loser ride in second. He smiled, remembering it was always Trey who got there first, that wild and impetuous teenaged kid that fate dealt a dead man's hand even before he had the chance to be a man. But that was back in the days just before they began to call themselves desperados. Those days were gone now for good, along with the best friend Johnny Blades had ever had.